KISSING THE ROADKILL
BACK TO LIFE

KISSING THE ROADKILL
BACK TO LIFE

A NOVEL

Gary M. Almeter

Attention schools and businesses: for discounted copies on large orders, please contact the publisher directly.

For information contact:
Unsolicited Press
Portland, Oregon
www.unsolicitedpress.com
orders@unsolicitedpress.com
619-354-8005

Cover Design: Andrew Almeter
Editor: S.R. Stewart

ISBN: 978-1-956692-18-1

Dedicated to the Malgosza, my favorite

"…..I wonder, little bubble

of unbudded capillaries, little one ever aswirl
in my vascular galaxies, what would you think

of this world which turns itself steadily
into an oblivion that hurts, and hurts bad?

Would you curse me my careless caressing you
into this world or would you rise up

and, mustering all your strength into that tiny throat
which one day, no doubt, would grow big and strong,

scream and scream and scream until you break the back of one
injustice,
or at least get to your knees to kiss back to life

some roadkill? I have so many questions for you,
for you are closer to me than anyone

has ever been, tumbling, as you are, this second,
through my heart's every chamber, your teeny mouth

singing along with the half-broke workhorse's steady boom and
gasp."

Ross Gay, *excerpted from* "Poem to My Child, If Ever You
Shall Be"

"Well let me tell you that it hurts so bad; it makes me feel so sad; it makes me hurt so bad."

Linda Ronstadt

My Son, the Taxidermist

Gloria listened as her hairdresser Judy described how her husband came into possession of the swordfish that now hung in Judy's family room; a swordfish which, if Gloria was hearing her correctly above the cacophony of the whirring, whooshing, rinsing, buzzing, of a hair salon on Saturday morning, was over six feet long from the end of its nose – or sword as it were – to its tail; with the Rhode Island state flag painted on the bulk of its body. Its nose pointed at the wall of Judy's kids' prom photos, First Communion photos, graduation photos, and wedding photos; its tail hovering above the head of whomever was sitting in the La-Z-Boy.

"I knocked his tuna off the wall, the one Frank caught when he won that fishing derby twenty, twenty-five years ago with the vacuum cleaner while I was vacuuming the drapes and Frank was all 'who vacuums the goddamn drapes?' and I was all 'the YouTube video says you can use the upholstery attachment for drapes and how about a fucking thank you for cleaning the drapes honey' but anyway the tuna's tail broke off when it hit the floor and so Frank took it down to his taxidermy place and who *has* a taxidermy place anyway to get it repaired or fixed and who knew that taxidermy repair shops even existed and so he sees this swordfish for sale and brings it home and I was all 'are you punishing me for knocking the damn tuna off the wall?' and he was all 'no they were practically giving it away' so Frank and I are friends again but I have this giant swordfish in the family room…"

Gloria closed her eyes and somewhere in between listening to Judy and the inevitable sleep that happened whenever she was under the hair dryer, she thought of her son, the taxidermist. How he goes to work and dons a leather apron and begins the process of disemboweling the animals and stuffing them with polyurethane foam. Or maybe he skins the animal and then affixes the skin to some sort of animal mannequin. Then he selects the perfect glass eyes and installs them in the form. Then he shellacs the whole thing with some sort of supersonic embalming varnish. He shellacs them with a special taxidermist's brush with special velvety supple bristles which pose no threat to the dead animal's epidermis. Maybe he specializes in a certain species; or a certain animal, she thought. Maybe he dwells in a coastal town just so that when fishermen from all over the world descend upon that coastal town for that coastal town's heralded blue marlin derby or big tuna invitational, they brought her their prize-winning catch to be expertly taxidermized. Or maybe his taxidermy practice has a more nefarious hue; maybe his bread and butter derives from taxidermizing endangered species like elephants and polar bears and giant pandas. Or maybe he is more of an artistic taxidermist and specializes in exotic birds, painstakingly replicating the feather pattern on large birds as he individually inserts them

My son is a marine biologist. My son is an auctioneer. My son is a violin prodigy. My son is a quarterback. My son is a pioneer. My son is a gambling addict. My son is a haberdasher. My son is a data analyst. My son is dignified. My son is a scoundrel. My son is a blogger. My son is a journalist. My son is a scrivener. My son is a detective. My son is a chief compliance officer. My son is an advertising executive. My son is a butcher. My son is a welder. My son is hypochondriac. My son is a cashier. My son is a heterosexual. My son is a rationalist. My son is a bad sport. My son is an angel. My son is a station agent."

There were times she stopped herself during these mental meanderings and musings and ask herself if the what he was mattered at all. He **was**. He existed. That he **was** was the important thing. She made him. He was living what she hoped was a good life. Is all the what of what he was of any consequence?

"My son is an honor student. My son is a molecular engineer. My son is an atheist. My son is a nurse. My son is a baker. My son is a dancer. My son is charismatic. My son is a photographer. My son is a tattoo artist. My son is a rock star. My son is a mathematician. My son is a tennis player. My son is a security guard. My son is imaginative. My son is polished. My son is a funeral director. My son is rustic. My son is an obstetrician. My son is a doctoral candidate. My son is humble. My son is a beekeeper. My son is humorous. My son is a genius. My son is a hermit. My son is a tennis player. My son is a waiter. My son is a lifeguard. My son is a competitive eater. My son is contemplative. My son is a college dropout. My son is a cross dresser. My son is a veteran. My son is an environmentalist. My son is a home economics teacher. My son is a kindergarten teacher. My son is a hazardous waste management analyst. My son is a subway and/or streetcar conductor. My son is a probation officer. My son is a tax attorney. My son is naïve. My son is colorful. My son is charming. My son is ebullient. My son is narrow minded. My son is a vegan. My son is sophisticated. My son is a retail store manager. My son is an exercise physiologist. My son is a procurement clerk. My son is a prosthetics technician. My son is a dry wall installer. My son is a Peace Corps Volunteer. My son is a huge fan of the opera. My son is an orthodontist. My son is a social worker. My son is a commercial fisherman. My son is devious. My son is a libertarian. My son is moody. My son is a baseball player. My son is extravagant. My son is a boilermaker. My son is a zoologist. My son is a Civil War reenactor. My son is a marathon runner. My son is a Dead head. My son is a film producer. My son is religious. My son is old-fashioned. My son is a hairstylist. My son is a Yankees fan. My son is a banker. My son is a follower. My son is a geologist. My son is a flamethrower. My son is absentminded. My son is a farmer. My son is a janitor. My son is a bus driver. My son is a disc jockey. My son is a postal worker. My son is witty. My son is a workaholic. My son is an optimist. My son is a barber. My son is a mountain climber. My son is a game show contestant. My son is a dog person. My son is a modernist."

There were times she stopped herself during these mental meanderings and musings and ask herself if the what he was mattered at all and think it all of no consequence; comforted by back then and something quite near a technological marvel allowing Brown students the opportunity to read newspapers from centuries ago. Maybe it wasn't a paper cut. Maybe one of the rolls of gelatinous microfiche film had come unspooled and sliced her buttocks. Either way it hurt.

The pluses outweighed the negatives though.

It felt good. He felt good.

He tasted good.

There was the one time that her boss stepped in some of JFK Jr.'s wayward semen. Gloria liked her boss and would have felt bad if he had slipped on JFK Jr.'s wayward semen and fell; but he hadn't fallen or even noticed it. It was like in the movies where the parents go away for a week and leave the kids at home and then the kids have a raucous party and have to clean up before the parents get home and in order to do so they have to fix holes in the kitchen and re-landscape and re-upholster most of the furniture and go to an antiques store to buy the perfect replacement for the broken vase and they do all this and then mom and dad get home and the kids notice a wayward beer bottle cap in plain sight and they worry that mom and dad will see it and all their efforts will be for naught but then mom and dad don't see it. It was like that.

It was a confidence booster. Not only did the knowledge that a sexy celebrity, though he was not yet the celebrity he would eventually become, wanted to have sex with her augment her self-esteem, the knowledge that she could be the aggressor was also something new. Something fun. A step towards self-actualization. Were one to do any sort of analysis on the sequence of events which led to their first tryst, one likely would conclude that she seduced him. Say, if the whole meeting were caught on surveillance footage and a body language expert – or cadre of body language experts – analyzed the footage, rewound it, replayed it, rewound it again, replayed it at a super-slow speed, rewound it again and zoomed in on hands and limbs and which limbs moved first and which limbs were positioned so and who leaned forward and who leaned backward and whose facial expressions belied some inner aggression and yearning and whose facial expressions exhibited surprise and willingness, the cadre of body language experts would almost certainly come to the conclusion that she initiated the first exchange. That she moved her mouth to meet his. That she slid her hand up his muddy shorts and removed his muddy rugby shirt.

They had also gotten mud on some of the equipment. October and November 1982 had been rainy months in Providence.

It was a confidence booster until it wasn't. She learned that hurt can corrode confidence thoroughly and with great alacrity.

She was just looking for some excitement. A declaration of independence. To capitalize and perhaps binge on the freedom of leaving Homer.

She had always considered the pregnancy a downside. A *negative*. But she got over that. Eventually. And her attitude about the whole thing changed in July 1999 when JFK Jr. died. And now that she was meeting her son, this new person, she realized the pregnancy was one of the good things.

The biggest downside though to having an affair with JFK Jr., one which she had not but perhaps should have anticipated while in the midst of the affair, was the feeling she'd have when it was done. There was the gnawing realization that she may have just had the best – the best man, the best lover, the best person, the best sex – she'd ever have. What does one even do for an encore? Maybe that is what happens at the end of any relationship. And everyone is certain they feel it the most.

PART I.

HOMER

BUTterfield 8

Her first name was Gloria, a name to which she could never quite get accustomed. It often seemed to her that her parents had someone else in mind when they named her. *Gloria* to her mind, was a name better suited to someone either impossibly pious or comically provocative. "Gloria" the name was both sultry and celestial; both angelic and lurid; both sacrosanct and seductive; it was Jim Morrison's too-fast G-L-O-R-I-A in the Doors's "Gloria" and the too-slow Glooooooooo-ooooo-oooo-ooooooooooo-ria of every church choir's "Angels We Have Heard on High." It was the name of and for someone perpetually stuck between two worlds, dipping proverbial toes into both, without ever fully committing to either.

This lack of cohesion was likely because her parents did have someone else in mind when they named her. Her parents named her after Elizabeth Taylor's character in *BUTterfield 8* which they had seen two nights before she was born, on November 28, 1960,

Her last name was Winegar, a name of German origin. And she hailed from good hearty corn-fed upstate New York stock. She lived in the same house from the day she was born until the day she moved to Providence save for the two years she spent living on campus at Syracuse University where her mother worked as a secretary.

Homer was as small as towns got. It had precisely one elementary school, one middle school, and one high school. It had two gas stations, one carwash, one deli and ice cream place, and the typical panoply of small shops which housed the auto mechanic, the welder, the upholsterer, the undertaker, some clergy, and the purveyor of lumber and hardware goods. It was a child's concept of a town, as though he or she built it from Lego. Everything you needed to live if your idea of living was more like subsisting than reveling in each brand new day.

She was one of 5955 Glorias born in the United States in 1960 making it that year's 79th most popular girl's name.

Her father, a genuinely good and kind man but simultaneously human nonetheless, and therefore generally powerless to be anything but human (flawed, carnivorous, reptilian, short sighted, astonishing, astounding humans) was smitten with Elizabeth Taylor, which seemed developmentally appropriate for a newly married 22-year-old young man in 1960. He was terrified of parenthood and, just one generation from an era when women were scarcely permitted to open bank accounts, did his very best being a husband and raising children.

Gloria's middle name was Hyacinth, chosen by her mother with neither input nor any threat of veto from Gloria's father. One of the negotiations of a marriage. Hyacinth was Gloria's maternal grandmother's name, a woman Gloria deeply loved. Hyacinth, as her name might suggest, loved flowers and knitting and crocheting and needlepoint and all things dainty.

Gloria's parents were called Dave and Connie. Dave's parents were farmers and he worked at the Smith Corona typewriter factory in Cortland, about 10 minutes south of Homer. Connie's parents were also farmers. She and Dave met in high school and married soon thereafter. Connie stayed home to raise Gloria and her sister Peggy and her brother David, Jr. until Dave Jr. was in school, and she took a job as a secretary at Syracuse University.

Naming a girl after someone synonymous with glamour will not necessarily or inevitably make the girl glamorous. Gloria was not glamorous, insofar as glamour is synonymous with sophistication and elegance and magnetism and fashionableness. Which is not to say that she was unattractive, quite the opposite. She was merely attractive in a no make-up, flowy sundress and sandals or blue jeans and sweatshirts, sort of way. She had almond eyes which alternated between greyish green and brownish grey and which sat appealingly and deeply on the perimeter of a round freckled face – freckles that could simultaneously say "these freckles make me sexy" and "these freckles make me a tomboy who has spent too much time in the sun likely playing beach volleyball with boys bigger than me." She was always tall for her age and when she stopped growing would be 5'10" and typically wore her chestnut hair in a short pixie-ish cut.

She fancied herself a confident person. She was determined, smarter than most, and nonchalant to the point of something resembling apathy with regard to appearance. She was athletic, played sports in high school. There was no shortage of suitors in high school and college and she lost her virginity under appropriate circumstances and at an appropriate age and navigated the world of sex and dating with aplomb. Her confidence helped with this.

She was fortunate to have a grandmother who fostered this confidence in her. Hyacinth once told her, "should a person take his or her thumbnail and scratch anyone's surface aggressively enough or just long enough, one would surely find that the least attractive in the world have, with a little tweaking, the capacity to be gorgeous while the most beautiful among us have, with just a few minor adjustments or unforeseen circumstances or minor deprivations, the potential to be among society's ugliest citizens." Of this she was certain and that certainty wended its way to Gloria.

Smith Corona

Her father began working at the typewriter factory a week after he graduated from high school. He began work on the assembly line, attaching letters to their respective levers and ribbon spools to their respective spool guides. After a few years he was promoted to calibrate the carriages and later, promoted to a supervisory role where he was tasked with maintaining and repairing the line itself.

When she was a girl he would often bring home the sub average or deformed and ultimately rejected typewriter keys, plastic keys with misshapen letters or something making them otherwise not up to Smith Corona standards. She would make necklaces and bracelets out of them with her friends' initials for her friends' birthdays. The family had a travel game where they would pick three or four or five letters (this number would increase as they got older) out of a Tupperware bowl kept at

Connie's feet. The Winegar kids would make a sentence using words that begin with those letters. For example, if Gloria picked up "G, P, L, B" her sentence could be "Gloria paints lavender birdhouses." Or something nonsensical like that. As long as it was a sentence. And rules would vary in terms of how liberally they could add pronouns and articles and other generic grammar staples.

Dave brought her a Super G electric typewriter a few weeks before she left for college. He told her he got it free because it had not passed quality control protocols, but Gloria suspected he had bought it outright, albeit with his employee discount. Kids know more about parents than parents realize. The typewriter, which Gloria still has, was an amazing turquoise color –unlike any color she had ever seen before she opened up the box; simultaneously nostalgic and futuristic; simultaneously dainty and powerful; simultaneously beautiful and industrial.

Gloria loved that her dad worked for a typewriter company – literally making typewriters. While he obviously viewed it as a job ("obviously" not because she ever discussed work with him but because men of a certain era have a very utilitarian way of looking at things) she thought about the words and documents that the typewriters he assembled produced. No one ever told her Gloria that Madeline L'engle hasn't written *A Wrinkle in Time* on a Smith Corona. Therefore, she must have. Same with Judy Blume, Scott O'Dell and later Stephen King and Patrick Michener.

Mary, Contrary

One winter, Gloria and her father went to the garage attic to retrieve the illuminated plastic Baby Jesus, Virgin Mary, St. Joseph and figures for their front yard Christmas display. They carried the plastic figures to the front yard along with the long outdoor extension cord and Dave knew just what to do in terms of knowing which ropes to tie around which figure to secure it to the stable. When they turned them on, the light which was to illuminate the virgin Mary was out so her dad went to the garage to get a new one and he asked Gloria to hold it while he unscrewed the burned out one but she dropped the good light in the snow and she said "Mother fucker" and her father looked at her, aghast, but then he started to laugh. And then she started to cry. And Gloria told him she was sorry and he said, and she would never forget this, "Do you know how funny it is to hear your daughter say motherfucker in front of the Virgin Mary?" And so Gloria started to laugh. And her dad told her not to tell her mother. And she had interpreted that as an irrevocable and perpetual license to curse whenever the fuck she wanted.

A Place in the Sun

When she was in 5th grade, her class went on a field trip to the Cortland Historical Museum, something they did every year.

Sometimes twice a year. And during another presentation on the climes of upstate New York and the importance of the lakes and the rivers and the engineering wherewithal it took to forge the Erie Canal, Gloria I audibly yawned – a practice of which she was rather fond in light of her disdain for her teacher, a woman named Miss Reiter. Gloria reveled in her ability to passively aggressively let Miss Reiter know that she, at ten years old, was vastly intellectually superior. Miss Reiter sternly nodded at a docent and then scoffed in her direction to signal that Gloria should be removed. Gloria told the docent that she was far more interested in current events – the assassinations of MLK and RFK and Jim Crow and Vietnam and the riots and the moon walking – than the importance of the then and still defunct Erie canal.

The docent took Gloria into a dimly lit room – or maybe it was just a room – and showed her some things upon which she was working: she had stacks of documents – timesheets, letters, train tickets, receipts.

"These are from the room Chester Gillette rented when he lived in Cortland working for his uncle's factory"

"Who's Chester Gillette?"

"I probably shouldn't say anything since you are just a kid."

"Then why would you put a stack of documents in front of me and tell me they were from Chester Gillette if you didn't want me to know who Chester Gillette was?"

"Good point" the docent said. And went on to tell Gloria about Chester Gillette, his devoutly religious west-coast upbringing and his move to Cortland to work in his uncle's skirt factory; how he had impregnated and was engaged to be married to another shirt factory worker named Grace Brown when he met Harriet Benedict, a wealthy Cortlandite who showed interest in him; how he eventually lured the still-pregnant Grace Brown to a lake in the Adirondacks; clubbed her to death with a tennis racket; was eventually caught, tried and executed.

Fifth-grade Gloria was intrigued.

She picked up some of the papers and saw a timesheet with Chester Gillette's signature on it. A real live murderer had once written his name on the page. It wasn't overly curvaceous or decorative; nor did it evince any predilections or propensity – at least none that she could tell – towards homicide; nor was it particularly tragic. What struck her was the ordinariness of it, just a name written on a timesheet. The docent said, "this was his last time sheet before he took Grace Brown to Big Bear Lake ostensibly for a vacation but really to kill her."

"What does ostensibly mean?"

"I'm sorry. It means you say – or maybe even think – you are doing something for one reason but really you are doing it for a different reason."

"Got it."

She loved seeing this document – this paper once beheld, once signed, by a murderer. A something to which he once afforded his attention. She loved that it was once in his home. That it might have been in his pocket; might have absorbed some of his perspiration as it sat in his pocket against his leg. Loved that the wrinkles might have come from him folding it or maybe they derived from his leg movements as it sat in his pocket. She thought that if we looked hard enough for some flourish or some inadvertent pencil markings or some overly aggressive cursive then she could ascertain some clue towards understanding the homicidal mind.

They spent twenty or thirty minutes in this back room, paging through documents used during the trial and transcripts of testimony. Gloria loved the documents, loved their smell and their fragility and the sound they made when flipped over. It was the docent's job to put them in these newly acquired and non-corrosive plastic sheets. And catalog them. She made it sound like drudgery. Gloria thought it sounded like a blast, imagining how future 5th graders, themselves bored with Miss Reiter's antiquated pedagogy, would one day find solace in knowing that the world was far more exciting than some would have you believe.

She was hooked. Then, when her mother started working in the library sciences department at S.U. and became friendly with the professors and at navigating the administrative hurdles that exist when your child is attending the university for free – it just seemed to make sense that she attends.

She was often asked as a library sciences major with a concentration in archives how she decided on such a major. The first time she answered that question she did so demurely and hesitantly, concerned she might sound like a sociopath, or worse, a nerd. She may have even been entertained the notion that there was something wrong with her. But it was in answering questions of this sort that she learned to own it. She learned that a person could say and do anything and make it be ok if it's done with confidence. So from then on, she did it confidently.

"I was really lucky in 5th grade when someone at Cortland historical museum took me to this room to see some of Chester Gillette's papers. I saw the value of the authenticity of the documents. I get to preserve history; imagine a baseball player holding Lou Gehrig's jersey; or a mechanic getting to drive Henry Ford's first Model T; or a haberdasher looking at Coco Chanel's first little black dress."

Confidence is really a learned behavior.

The chance meeting with the docent served the rare double purpose of a) cementing her vocation and b) cementing her affinity for Elizabeth Taylor who portrayed the wealthy socialite who became Montgomery Clift's muse in "A Place in the Sun" – Hollywood's take on the story of Chester Gillette.

She came to believe that she resembled Ms. Taylor; likely more than she actually did.

Decades later, an art student at the Rhode Island School of Design, visiting the Brown Univeristy library, would tell her that she was the spitting image of Berthe Marisot from Edouard Manet's "Berthe Marisot with a Bouquet of Violets." She would thank him and when she was done with her work, would locate a book of Manet paintings and, with a bit of trepidation, find this Berthe Marisot person and upon finding her, would concur, perhaps a bit enthusiastically, with the art student.

Gary M. Almeter

The Non-Apple Queen's Gambit

Gloria was not a tomboy but generally eschewed the things in which other girls reveled. She never liked dolls and while her aunts and grandparents gave them to her with some frequency for her birthday and Christmas, she never had the audacity to discard them. She never considered being cheerleader. There was also this apple festival near Homer that crowned an apple queen, a senior in high school, every October after a number of talent and gown competitions, and while she had been encouraged to enter the pageant, told she was a shoe-in even by several teachers concerned with such things, she never seriously considered doing so. She said to her dad, "I just don't want to be the apple queen." And he had replied, "Then don't."

She played volleyball in high school because she was both tall and really good at it. One year the Homer High School team made it to the state semi-finals.

There were days in high school when she would look into a mirror to check her face or to make sure the part in her hair was straight or just to see if anything more sinister was afoot, like nostril hairs or the early stages of a unibrow or a blemish and she would stared at herself at close range – watching her pupils dilate and examining all the flecks and specks and gradations in her irises and making shapes with her mouth and furrowing her brow and seeing what the furrowing did to the shape of her eyes and contemplating whether the length of her eyelashes was appropriate or if her nostrils were too big and if her nose was proportionate to her face and what color her lips were and what color her eyes were. She did this for hours when

47

she was a girl. Sometimes she was positively certain that she was a knockout; other times fancying herself as revolting as a girl could get; sometimes fully hoping and expecting herself to morph into something more beautiful just by sheer will and patience and just by wishing it to be so. Do all women do this? Wonder if they are pretty? Wonder for hours if they are pretty? Seek certainty in their wonderment? Marvel at their seemingly limitless imperfections? Be awed by a feature or two that we really like. She wondered. She had a little speck of bright yellow in her left iris. Or maybe it's her right one. She was always looking at herself in a mirror when she saw it. She was surprised at every new blemish or freckle or whisker. Do they portend and prognosticate about how their features will evolve into what they will and should become – like how all the continents that were once all fused together as that supercontinent Pangaea split apart and floated into where they are now to form the world as we know it? Did she read something once that said the eyeballs with which we are born are the eyeballs we have for the rest of our lives? Like they don't grow or shrink or anything? But it seems like they can change color and shape and maybe the eye holes (is there a name for those – eye sockets) can shift and get further apart from one another and meander around the face. It wasn't easy being a girl. Even harder to be a girl who is trying to be herself.

Gary M. Almeter

Pistachio Formica

Gloria began to feel it when she was fourteen, feel that there existed this momentum in the world – perhaps natural perhaps manufactured – which propelled people in a way that seemed almost predetermined. It was at 14 she realized that it is more difficult than she had always been taught for a person to change courses. Her dad would come home from work and the five of them would sit down to dinner when someone would ask him what was new at the factory, and he would report on his co-workers' triumphs: engagements and baptisms and weddings and new homes and new cars and his co-workers' challenges: foregoing braces for the kids because they couldn't afford them and snow mobile accidents and hunting accidents and sick pets and the what have you. Gloria began to notice that her dad often reported that children of his colleagues got jobs at the factory after high school. Kids not much older than her, kids with whom she had shared hallways and cafeteria space at the high school, working third shift in the smelting department or in shipping and receiving where they would stay for the next few decades. It was at age fourteen when she began to detect the disparity between the expectations of those with whom her mother worked and the expectations of those with whom her father worked. During those family meals, when her father was done reporting on his day, as her mother would tell the family about hers. Connie's reportage was peppered with the things important to mothers – the kimmelweck rolls on which she made her roast beef sandwich for lunch were both really, really tasty and on sale; a deer ran across the highway on her way home from work and she had to quickly apply – though definitely not slam – her brakes or else she would have hit the poor thing; and Shirley never remade the coffee in the departmental kitchenette coffee maker after she poured herself the last cup. Her mom reported on the news of her own day. She was elated when the department bought her an electric typewriter though it took her a while to get used to it. Her world was the shaded area of a Venn diagram where academia and office supplies meet. Professor so and so had an article to send out but they were out of carbon paper and she would have to retype it on that special mimeograph paper and he was unhappy with the size of her footnotes and meanwhile she had students (some of whom would not have known what manners were if manners came up to them and hit them upside the head with a two by four) and then Barbara from across the hall would call in sick and Jane should be more conscientious of where she blew her second hand smoke and it was rumored that Edie and Professor Wallinsky were having an affair. She was elated when Liquid Paper began to come in different shades. She was livid when during the construction of the Carrier Dome she had to park an extra block and a half away from her building. Such emotion prompted by such mundanity! Gloria thought the whole thing sad.

She also began to notice that the children of professors for whom her mother worked had different trajectories than the children of people with whom her father worked. They went to private schools in the Syracuse area and when they were done at those schools they went to college. And they went to college at places like Stanford and Yale and MIT and the University of Michigan and the University of Virginia and Harvard.

It was less an epiphany than a gradual realization that there were two very different worlds, her parents firmly ensconced in the one in which paying for braces and a new car with power windows and a new above-ground pool and a new typewriter and colored Liquid Paper were celebrated. Others ensconced in a world where expectations were much higher.

When she was 14 her parents had a party for her sister's First Communion and they set up picnic tables in the garage and borrowed large industrial sized coffee makers and some folding chairs from the church and asked people to bring side dishes — jello molds and three bean salads and potato salads — and then set hot plates and crock pots and coffee makers on top of Dave's tool bench and plugged them into outlets which typically powered his circular saws and that light he used when he worked underneath their cars; they filled a kiddie pool with ice and Nehi sodas and Genesee beer. Gloria would ask herself, "what are we saying when we have parties in the garage? Are we telling people that we do not want them dropping cake on our carpeting and burning holes in our upholstery with their lazy cigarettes made lazier by the cans of Genesee beer that we serve in the large inflatable pool we borrowed from cousin Jerry and filled with ice? Were we telling people that we couldn't afford to set up a tent in the back yard? Or caterers? Or that this event just didn't warrant a tent? Or maybe we were embarrassed by those things that were inside our house. The dated furniture and the pistachio-colored Formica counters. Or maybe we were reveling in our blue collar-ness. Maybe what we were saying is

51

that since we work so hard during the week we are not going to do anything to create more work on weekends. We are not embarrassed by the outdated shag carpet nor do we really give a shit if Uncle Albert drops a Pall Mall onto it (or into it). We just don't want to clean up after the party. And guess what else? We are going to use disposable flatware and plates and napkins. We are going to splurge on plastic forks and spoons and knives and we will even splurge and buy napkins that say 'First Holy Communion' on them and see that big-ass Rubbermaid garbage can over there? You can throw all of that shit right in there because we are not washing dishes today."

Maybe that is what they were saying. Maybe they were reveling in their own way. Maybe they were declaring themselves independent of even one more modicum of extra work.

These questions, along with all the strange new smells of classmates' perspiration and deodorants and acne cleansers and toners and lotions and creams and the petri dish that is an 8th grade classroom, made her 14th year an especially confusing time.

Additionally, just before she turned fourteen, her aunt took her to see a movie called "Benji" about a stray bit scrappy dog who helps save a pair of orphans from kidnappers. A few months later, she and some friends went to see a movie called "The Texas Chainsaw Massacre" about a chainsaw massacre that happens in Texas.

So that is what being 14 was like – whiplash as the world changes from Benji to Texas Chainsaw Massacre.

Gary M. Almeter

The Epileptic Hitchhiker

When Gloria turned sixteen she got her learner's permit, which meant that she got to spend hours in the car with her dad as he taught her how to drive: parallel parking between cones set up in the church parking lot; driving in silence so as not to be distracted by the radio or the conversation for hours through windy country roads and then one day trying the highway; driving on icy parking lots to know what to do in a skid. Her dad also made sure she learned how to change a tire and how to use a flare gun and how to change oil. She dreaded these lessons but as soon as she got her driver's license she wished could do it all over again because it turned out it was sort of fun and her dad knew what he was talking about when it came to all that stuff.

There was this one day when she and her dad were driving around, and she stopped without warning to pick up a hitchhiker, a man named Danny who went to their church and who had to go to the drugstore thrice a week to get his epilepsy medication. Her dad didn't say anything as she chatted with Danny in the back seat as they drove to the drugstore. Her dad didn't say anything as Danny got out of the car and walked into the drugstore and she pulled out of the parking lot and back onto West Main Street. A few minutes went by with nothing being said until Gloria said, "Do unto others as you would have them do unto you. Right?" It was probably the most rebellious thing she had ever done.

Orange You Glad?

Gloria went to Syracuse University because her mother worked as a secretary there for several professors in the University's School of Library Science Department though when Gloria attended it was called the more sophisticated sounding School of Information Studies. She got a BS in library science with a concentration in archives and preservation.

She lived on the Syracuse campus for her freshman and sophomore years but since room and board were not included in the tuition remission program for university employees, her parents had to pay for it. Which turned out to be rather tough for them. The years she spent living at Syracuse University were very fun. But the strain it had on her parents and sister and brother seemed unfair. So she commuted to Syracuse the remaining two years.

She had an internship at the Women's Rights Museum in Seneca Falls her senior year anyway. She was tasked with cataloging recently unearthed letters of Elizabeth Cady Stanton.

A Conversation on the Steps of George Washington Hall at Phillips Academy Andover

"I really don't like Elvis."

"Dude have some respect. He just died."

"I'm aware of the fact that he's deceased, Chuck. I'm just saying that I do not care for him."

"You can't say that."

"I can't say it? Or I can't think it?"

"You definitely can't say it. And since you have to like Elvis, you might as well get accustomed to not thinking it."

"I don't have to like Elvis."

"Yes. You do."

"Do not."

"Sorry, John. You do."

"I don't. But why are you taking the position that I must?"

"Look man. I don't make the rules. I will likely make the rules someday. But for now, I do not. And you're John Fitzgerald Kennedy, Jr. You have to like America. You have to like American things. You have to like all the American things lest you be reviled. You have to like the things for which America is known. You have to revel in America. You have to drip, ooze, and sweat America. You just do."

"Or what, Chuck? And who says 'lest'?"

"Or you'll get crucified. Come on, man. America's favorite son thinks he's too good for American things? That doesn't play well."

"Me not liking Elvis has nothing to do with geography. Or for that matter, his appearance or his penchant for peanut butter and bananas and tranquilizers or any of the other things on which he dined. I just don't like his music."

"I understand that. But many do not. And people you know...."

"...you know....?"

"....You know."

"I don't know."

"They like to see people, you know, knocked down a few pegs."

"So me not liking Elvis – and let me straight with you Chuck, I loathe Elvis. He's disgusting; he can't sing a goddamned note; nonetheless all his songs sound the same, whether it's 'Amazing Grace' or 'Hound Dog'; to that end he is unable to distinguish between the divine and the rancorous; he's gaudy. And he can't act. – has less to do with me having to uphold a certain patriotism and more to do with people's enthusiasm to see me....what, get knocked down a few pegs?"

"It's probably a blend of both."

"Got it."

"Again, I don't make the rules here John."

"I know. If you made the rules, Elvis would replace Hamilton on the $10 bill?"

"Who uses $10 bills?"

"I appreciate your concern. But look, if we extend your hypothesis..."

"It's not a hypothesis."

"...to its logical conclusion, then me preferring Peter Gabriel over Phil Collins becomes some sort of assessment or judgment or preference on tall people versus short people. Like if I tell someone I like Peter Gabriel more than Phil Collins, then they can assume that I'm what.... Anti-bald?"

"One need only look at your hair to know you're anti-bald."

"All I'm saying is that people like what they like. Why do people have to attach a value to it?"

"Again."

"I know. You don't make the rules."

"That's right, John."
"Alright Chuck. Let's go eat."

The Saffron Omega

There came a time, somewhere during one of her commutes to Syracuse during her senior year in college, when the streets and the sounds and the cadence and every single thing about her hometown started to feel oppressive. When she thought if she had to navigate the grocery store parking lot one more time or have to wait for the green arrow to turn left onto West Main Street or wait in line at the grocery store while the cashier chats to the customer ahead of her about Watergate or watercress or water in her basement that she would just go fucking bonkers. She had always known, or at least since she could remember, she would leave Homer someday but then the day came when she was to leave and she felt guilty for ever finding it oppressive and contemplating a life in Homer. It was a fine place to live; fine enough for her parents and for many of the people with whom she went to high school, some of whom had even started working with her dad at the Smith Corona factory.

But then her supervisor at the Women's History Museum called about a job at Brown University and she applied and her favorite professor wrote a great recommendation and she bought a new suit and drove to Providence and interviewed and the job was what she always wanted and she got the job and all of a sudden it was time to move.

August 1982 had been a hot one in Homer and by the time she had orchestrated the packing of most of her earthly possessions into the 1979 Oldsmobile Omega her parents had given her for graduation, the shirt and shorts she was planning on wearing for the trip were soaked with sweat, which meant that she would have to find something new to wear, which meant borrowing something from her sister since all her clothes were packed.

She stopped scurrying and orchestrating and packing and cursing under her breath to accept a glass of iced tea from her mother as they discussed what to do. She took some deep breaths and endeavored to identify what exactly she was feeling since up to that point all conversations and thoughts concerned moving logistics – routes and gas mileage and conversations about trunk space. Something happens to a person when they pack all of their earthly possessions in to a 1979 Oldsmobile Omega. She felt pride in her engineering acumen. She felt a certain solace in knowing that all that she valued was secure and visible and sufficiently accounted. She felt a little befuddled in seeing the sum of her life distilled into the cubic space of the 1979 Oldsmobile Omega. To her dad, the gift of a car was the best gift a father could give a daughter. He loved the car with an intensity that is both symptomatic of an intense American Dream worldview and profoundly, though oddly, endearing. The enormity of what was about to happen almost hadn't hit her yet; she knew it was imminent but could not quite picture the Oldsmobile Omega would soon be cruising, a reference to both the size of the car and her father's affinity for the cruise control feature – a new luxury he was determined to engage at every opportunity – and the size of the Oldsmobile Omega, behind her father and mother in their own 1980 Pontiac Bonneville packed with its own cargo – mostly domestic items from a shopping spree Gloria and her mom had at Ames Department Store, over the New York State thruway towards its ultimate destination of Providence, RI.

Her parents helped her and annoyed her. She was tired and nervous and angry at herself for being annoyed with them but she also chuckled to herself because the Oldsmobile Omega was brown and she was travelling to a job at Brown University and how fucking silly was that. Then she thought of all the times her mother called the Oldsmobile Omega "Brown Betty" in front of your friends and how embarrassed she her family named cars; and all the times her father corrected her mother and jokingly though also a little bit proudly reminded her that the color of the Oldsmobile Omega was actually Saffron Firemist and how he officiously, in his best game show host voice, cited to the catalog that the Chevrolet dealer in town, who was also her father's friend and fellow parishioner and old high school buddy and overall good guy, gave him which had a whole page of the color swatches available for the 1979 Oldsmobile Omega.

When you live in a small town so much depends on a car. The racing home to beat curfew, the fumbling in the back seat with boys who up-to-then had thought they knew what they were doing, the trips to the mall, the parking in the fields to drink after the football games.

Then she reverted to genuine befuddlement at how all those years of folding the corners of the JCPenney catalogs while creating her lists for Santa and all those trips to the big shopping malls in Syracuse and all the Syracuse University sweatshirts she bought and all the dresses and accessories she bought for college dances and all the sneakers and shoes and sunglasses and earrings and perfumes and cassette tapes and stuffed animals and pillows and all the accoutrements of adolescence and girlhood and young womanhood when condensed, fit into one car. And while was feeling all that she watched her father strain to fit the toaster oven her mother bought during the trip to Ames into the back seat of his Pontiac Bonneville and watched as he struggled to secure it atop the boxes of dinnerware her mom also bought her and she knew he was concerned about the box with the toaster oven obstructing his view from the rear view mirror, probably overly concerned, but that was just what he did and then he cursed, not a $64,000 curse but the more innocuous "you son of a bitch" which was absolutely appropriate.

She felt guilty for making them do this – packing up all her shit and struggling and cursing to drive her to a city five hours away because she felt like escaping and she paused then to consider "escaping what?" because they had been great parents and moving felt like a rebuke. She felt guilty for all the nights she went out with friends during breaks from school and over the summer and how she spent the money she earned from her summer job as a lifeguard on clothes and cassette tapes while they scrimped and saved and she felt guiltier still for all the times she rolled her eyes at them when they asked her to get off the phone and for all the times she sat down at the dinner table, saw another pot roast, and said something that evinced her dearth of enthusiasm for pot roast. But then she recalled how proud her dad seemed at church last week telling the Kirkmans and the Dinsmores and the Pantagionis and the Ratchfords about how he wouldn't be at mass next weekend because they would all be in Providence getting Gloria settled in so she could start her new job. She was astonished that her pillows and a goose down comforter and towels and bathmats occupied all of the trunk space in her parents' 1980 Bonneville and she was certain that, if asked, her father would know the amount of trunk space in cubic feet to the nearest hundredth because that was just who Dave was. She saw her mom scurrying back and forth between the cars and the kitchen offering iced tea; she noticed her dad winced every time the screen door slammed closed and she knew that he felt his own guilt at having a screen door with such insufficient tension in its springs and hinges that it slammed and what the neighbors must have thought of them. She heard her mom tell her brother and sister to behave while they are gone. She felt pride at the relationships she had with them after years of adversarialness. She felt relief when she remembered that her parents would be doing the same thing in a few weeks when they took her brother to begin his freshman year at Syracuse and so the trauma of this day would soon be diminished or diluted if not altogether eviscerated.

Her dad was visibly and audibly winded from packing the towels and the toaster oven and the sheets and the area rugs and the blender and the pots and pans into the car and her mom continued to scurry back and forth between the car and the kitchen with apples and granola bars and cans of Nehi soda for the trip and asked Gloria how many apples she wanted and if she wanted grape Nehi or orange Nehi and her brother and sister were in the living room arguing about whose turn it was to wash the dishes and generally being miscreants even though they just promised their mother and father they would behave for the one evening they would be gone and Gloria knew she would miss the comfort of it all, the familiarness of it and the ordinariness of it. Maybe it was ok to be ordinary she thought. But then she remembered all those times she overheard the cashier talk about Watergate or Water cress or the water in her basement and she understood and knew for certain it was time to leave.

One last look at the house. She pulled out of the driveway from which she had made egress thousands of times previously, past the stores, past the park, past the school, past Mrs. Looney's house and the houses of the Schmidts and the Dyers and the Bergerons and the Drakes and the Hubbards and the Kirsches and the Litzenbergers and the Macks and the Vosburgs.

On to new adventures.

PART 2

PROVIDENCE

Benevolent Street

She rented an apartment on the third floor of a bright yellow
three-story house on a street called Benevolent Street. The
house had a turret and while her apartment, about half of the
third floor, did not occupy the turret, her bedroom abutted the
turret and so had a very cool rounded wall. She loved the round
wall; love that she lived on a street called Benevolent Street;
loved meeting her neighbors, a couple Brown University
graduate students, a single professor, and an artist of some kind,
who was home all the time. The whole thing made her feel very
grown up. The apartment itself had a sepia tone – which isn't
to say that it was dreary or lacked adequate illumination – by
virtue of the way the sunlight hit and bounced off the windows
and onto the hardwood floors and the plaster walls and wood
crown moldings and gave the apartment an antique hue. The
kitchen was green and the bathroom was pink.

Gloria had a few days before she was to report to new
employee orientation. She and her parents unpacked, found a
department store (so disorienting when department stores, gas
stations, convenient stores, fast food places all have different
names, different facades, different colored signs from those to

which you are accustomed; she felt like Lewis & Clark negotiating this new terrain) to buy stuff they forgot or couldn't get until they measured things in Gloria's apartment, shower curtain, window shades, runners, area rugs, and Gloria's dad spent the afternoon installing hooks for coats and towel racks and curtain rods and attaching, affixing, caulking, tightening, securing, and generally fixing things. Her mom lined all her kitchen drawers with contact paper and put her spices in the cupboard and cleaned the refrigerator crispers and washed the windows and at some point in the afternoon, before they went out to buy a bed and a sofa and arrange for delivery later that week, Gloria thought "my God how hard it must be a parent to raise a child only to have that child leave and they can't just leave on their own they have to *still* rely on you for every damn thing."

That night they ate at one of the Italian restaurants in Providence's robust Little Italy and it was a clear Saturday summer night so restaurants and sidewalks were crowded and everyone was having fun and the whole city seemed to glow and pulse and Gloria was elated. They got ice cream – gelato they called it at the Italian dessert place and Dave asked the man at the counter what was the difference between ice cream and gelato and found the Italian man's reply incomprehensible so just shrugged and walked outside because that is what dads do when confronted with the notion that their world is changing and that from now on their daughters will be eating gelato and saying fancy words like "soda" instead of "pop." Then the three of them, Gloria and her parents, went back to the apartment and slept on the floor. Soundly.

The next day, before the parents drove home, they walked to the library where Gloria would be working, the John Hay library, a massive gray stone building adjacent to the main Rockefeller Library. They took a picture of Gloria standing at the entrance. As they drove away Gloria regretted all the times she rolled her eyes or huffed or replied a little too tersely when her mom asked her something like "where should we install the Dustbuster?" or her dad asked, "how high do you want this coat rack?" Gloria spent the next few days driving around the city, doing a dry run of her walk to work, unpacking, ironing, and generally getting acclimated to her new environs.

Friday was new employee orientation.

Ruth

Ruth was hired to work at Women & Children's Hospital of Rhode Island, affiliated with the Warren Alpert Medical School of Brown University and, to make extra money, the Brown University Student Health Services in the Andrews Building at 13 Brown Street, so she was therefore an employee of Brown University and therefore required to attend the Brown University new employee orientation in Sayles Hall in August 1982 where, by virtue of the fact they happened to be waiting in the same line to get their identification cards laminated at the same time, met Gloria. And because they happened to be waiting in the identification card lamination line together, the last step in a day-long series of processes that included employee handbook distribution, employee eligibility verification, health insurance selection, dental insurance selection, they began talking, each expressing their exhaustion and the inherent frustration that comes from new employee orientation, and the talking led to laughing and more chatting – the innocuous chatting in which women in their twenties waiting in line for new employee identification card lamination engage – and decided to go to dinner that evening.

Ruth, already twenty-three, was from the Jamaica Plain neighborhood of Boston. She was about as tall as Gloria with a rounder face and a slight Jamaican accent; she had longer hair that even at new employee orientation she wore in a high messy bun; a bun that said, "I sit atop the head of a woman on the go." It was a fun bun, and while it appeared effortless, was also sufficiently tidy and secure to alert people that Ruth meant business.

Neither Ruth nor Gloria were familiar with Providence, a big city that is really a small town which had seen better days, and they decided to have dinner at a place near campus so they could walk. Their discussion that night meandered between the mundane and the profound (why did you move to Providence – what were your favorite movies – who was your most significant relationship – what was your family like – favorite bands and concerts and songs – who were your friends at home – what was college like – what do you hope to get out of the job – describe your parents – siblings? – grandparents – what do parents do for a living? – they both hated bars like this one – they both hated pub food – so why did they even come here – nicknames – favorite pets – chosen career paths – hopes and dreams.) They ate nachos and chicken fingers. It was Friday so they could sleep in the next day and, because they were young and frightened and exhausted and generally lamenting the fact that they were basically adults, had too much to drink. So they walked to Gloria's apartment, singing "Gloria" by Laura Branigan as they walked down Benevolent Street. Ruth spent the night and when she said she had to throw up, Gloria held her unbunned hair as she vomited an evening's worth of wine and nachos into Gloria's pink toilet and they likely woke up her new neighbors but neither one cared.

Something happens when people throw up together. It creates an instant friendship.

Work

That following Tuesday she began her job as a manuscripts archivist at Brown University's John Hay library. She had an office in the basement, a subterranean office, where she worked on both chronicling and protecting and stabilizing and archiving Brown's special collections – the Civil War manuscripts collection, the letters of T.S. Eliot, ther letters of Frederick Douglass, the Sergei Khrushchev papers, original Henry Davod Thoreau manuscripts - while also managing their distribution to eager, ardent, self-important Brown students. Besides summer jobs and her internship, it was her first full-time job. And certainly her first professional job, one where she had to navigate the politics of work, the employee refrigerator, the coffee maker, her boss's moods; learning the workplace policies and protocols and rules, which of all the elucidated rules were compulsory, which discretionary, which positively optional, which of the spoken rules yielded implicit rules and which of which rules each particular rule enforcer was particularly fond.

She had a few days of library-specific orientation; learning about library policies, library equipment, phone policies and protocols, break times, restroom locations. Gloria would be responsible for her own discreet section of the special collections desk in the basement. She would spend most of her days of this first year cataloging the family papers of American educational reformer and Whig politician Horace Mann. Part of cataloging old papers involves inserting them into protective sleeves to shield them from ultraviolet light and water and the oily residue from fingerprints. Whenever someone came to the desk with a question or request, she was tasked with assisting them.

She would have to work a few night shifts per week; which were simultaneously required and voluntary; required insofar as John Hay reference librarians had to work at least an additional 8 hours so that there was someone at the archives desk every minute that the library was open; and voluntary insofar as archivists could choose which nights and which weeknights he or she worked; they could work 8 extra hours, 12 extra hours, 16 extra hours, or even 20 extra hours; though administrators discouraged them from working more than 20. There was a stipend for these hours so they considered them both a luxury and a burden.

Questions and requests typically came from undergraduate students, usually upperclassmen, tasked with an in-depth research project or final thesis which required original research from primary sources. The John Hay Library had letters and papers and collected documents of a host of politicians, founding fathers, abolitionists, generals, inventors, scientists, philosophers, societies, foundations, families, explorers, writers, industrialists, zoologists, and general people of interest. Gloria was responsible for distributing and maintaining and lending collections house din the basement.

Primary sources included newspapers and periodicals and there were hundreds of years of hundreds of newspapers in the basement also. Usually on microfilm or microfiche. Part of Gloria's job included helping people find relevant articles and spooling them onto the appropriate viewing machine.

The Facts of Life

The first thing she noticed about him was not his hair or his gait or his abs or his legs – it was his pores. He had the clearest most beautiful pores of any human being who has ever lived. She was certain of it. Notice isn't even the right word. Notice is what happens when you see that the people who live in the house down the block have trimmed their shrubs; or hung baskets of geraniums on their front porch; or got a new car; or one of those things around which you wrap a garden hose; or had hung up their Christmas lights. It registers in your cortex and then dissipates. Seeing JFK Jr.'s pores was less an act of anatomical perception and more akin to the first time a musician hears Beethoven's 9th Symphony; or a painter viewing Van Gogh's *Starry Night* for the first time; or a poet, the first time he reads Walt Whitman's *Song of Myself.* It was art. He was art. His face was art. Once she was able to wrap her mind around the existence of his pores, that it was metaphysically possible for such pores to *be* on a member of the human species, she then became capable of perceiving his hair and his abs and his legs and his gait. This was also largely due to the fact that it was evening, one of the evenings she was tasked with working until the library closed, and she was engrossed in a magazine, and that he had to clear his throat and say "Excuse me" to get her attention. When she looked up to identify the man who needed help with the archives, she saw his face first, his face was literally inches from hers. Had she seen him approach the research desk she may have noticed his gait or his hair. Had he been shirtless she likely would have noticed his abs. Though since shirts and shoes were required in the library, this would have been doubly alarming. Presumably the experience of seeing JFK Jr. for the first time is different for everyone. Grandmothers still talk about seeing him salute his dad at the dad's funeral, televised and watched by the nation. She will talk about seeing him at the reference desk for as long as she lives.

At least that is how it was for Gloria when he approached the archives desk at the library that evening in September. Some zillion thoughts went through her mind, one of them of course the part of new employee orientation where the lady from human resources sort of haphazardly told all new employees that a romantic relationship with students was absolutely prohibited; haphazardly not because it was unimportant but because it was assumed, one of the tenets of work; one of the tenets of dwelling in a functioning society.

After JFK Jr. said, "excuse me," she thought she heard him say something about Horace Mann and education. His voice was simultaneously deep and comfortingly lilting; he delivered the words he spoke with both kindness and assurance; and he pronounced those words intentionally, as though each one had been personally retrieved from the depths of his big bottomless heart.

Had she known he was a student there? Of course. Everyone knew that. Had she prepared herself for meeting him? No. Was it possible to prepare oneself for that? No. Brown University was not unacquainted with celebrity. One of Klaus von Bulow's stepchildren went there; as did Amy Carter and a Mondale son; and Felice Schachter, one of the girls from the original *Facts of Life* was there too. At orientation, the human resources lady had briefly told the new hires that celebrities and celebrity children were not to be treated any differently than the other students.

The human resources lady had clearly not ever seen or been approached by or spoken to JFK Jr.

Gloria took a deep breath and, determined to be professional, managed a positively innocuous "Good evening. What can I help you with?"

"I'm doing some research for a paper on educational reform, both for a class and for a project on which I'm working related to a new school in East Harlem, and I need to look at some things in the Horace Mann collection. The librarian upstairs told me they were down here."

"Got it," she managed as she leaned across the desk to grab the binder with the index of all the collections and their specific locations. "Yes sir. The Horace Mann papers are back here. Shelved back there" inelegantly motioning towards the back room work area with her chin. "What can I help you find?"

He handed her a list of documents he had identified and written out on a piece of notebook paper. Her thjumb grazed his as she took the list. She examined the list and told him she could have most of the documents ready for him the next day. When he left, she held the list to her face, sniffed it, touched the letters, touched the frayed edges, examined his handwriting - the curls and the slants and the spacing of the letters. The boyishness of it was jarring he seemed to dot his lowercase "i"s with authority and make his uppercase "I"s with delicacy; he crossed his lowercase "t"s with a unique and highly appealing dash. He blended cursive writing with block printing and there were lines where his palm smudged some of the ink and she was astounded by both the magnificence and ordinariness of it all.

And His Breath Smelled Like Cardamom

Over the next few weeks they discussed and researched and delved into archives.

One evening in October, he was standing behind her as she pointed out the shelf upon which she placed the binders containing Mann's 1846 papers. At some point as she described the state of his correspondence with Elizabeth Palmer Peabody regardoing temperance, JFK Jr. breathed on her. His breath touched her neck. Later she would tell Ruth, "It felt just as you might think it felt – like the cool breezes of the alps with Maria von Trapp singing on the top of the mountain and echoing through the village. But it was also minty. And smelled like cardamom. With notes of vanilla. I'm not even joking."

"How did he get his breath to smell like cardamom?" Ruth asked.

"I don't know. But he did. He does."

"Is there a cardamom gum that rich Caucasians chew?"

"That's an excellent question. The answer to which I do not know."

"Maybe it's a Greek thing. He lived in Greece for a while, right?"

"I think that's right." Gloria said, surprised by her level of certainty with respect to an answer of which she was not certain.

"Are there Secret Service guys with him?"

"None that I can see."

"I guess that's why they call them 'secret'."

"Do you think if he put a piece of cardamom gum in his mouth and a secret service guy said, 'hey can I get a piece of that cardamom gum?' he'd be allowed to give him a piece or do you think it's prohibited?"

"Why would sharing gum be prohibited?"

"I don't know."

The conversation went on like that. Ruminations on secret Caucasian gum flavors and Secret Service protocols and Manhattan orthodontists.

The night his breath touched the back of her neck was a Tuesday evening. JFK Jr. wore nylon shorts that were somehow both muddy and iridescent and a collared rugby shirt and loafers with no socks. "Men of a certain pedigree wear collared shirts even when they are exerting themselves and pushing themselves to the limit on the rugby field," she thought to herself. He drew near to the archives desk with a smile and with just enough of a scent to render him human but not so strong and invasive a scent as to render him revolting. Even his sweat smelled great; not like cardamom. Not like any discernible spice; but good nonetheless.

They chatted for a bit, by now acquainted with one another, "How was your day, Gloria?" "It was good, how was yours?" she would have replied. She might have also punctuated her reply with a mature and sophisticated giggle; definitely not a submissive patronizing cute giggle but a giggle nonetheless. "Oh it was fine." he would have answered demurely. They likely discussed that semester's theater production in which he had the lead and his rugby. He set a stack of books on the shelf and told her he had identified some new primary source materials from the from the Massachusetts Board of Education reports. She went back to the microfiche stacks and located them and brought a few envelopes and boxes filled with the brownish aubergine gelatinous microfiche sheets and said, "Let's get started."

Typically, students were not permitted behind the archives desk. The archivist would locate the article requested by the student and print it out. Such printouts were ten cents per sheet and because of the disparities between print size and newspaper size and the general guesswork each archivist employed when printing out the articles, a single article could run a student up to $3.50. Often, the student would pay this only to discover the article was not even relevant or helpful for their research. So it was common practice for the archivists – during evening hours when the library directors were at home – to let students behind the archive desk and identify those pages they wanted printed and how. So when she invited John back to the microfiche machine, it was not *that* defiant an act. She threaded the microfiche sheet through the machine and positioned it so that the First Annual report of the Board of Education was visible on the display. John stood behind her, leaned over her chair, and started reading – skimming really – the article.

At one point when he was reading about teacher training, she felt his breath on her neck.

"Have you ever seen one of those commercials about what it felt like to bite into a York Peppermint Pattie?" She would later, after she finally told her, ask Ruth.

"Jesus his breath again."

"Yep. As I sat at the microfiche machine and felt John Kennedy Junior's breath on my neck. It was like the experiences in the York Peppermint Patty commercials – when the guy on the crowded subway train bites into a York Peppermint Pattie and suddenly feels like he is standing alone and triumphant on the top of a snowy mountain – except better. Take the York Peppermint Patty experience and add other experiences to it – riding a wooden roller coaster at Coney Island, walking over the Brooklyn Bridge, strolling through Paris in a moon lit evening after dining on Parisian meats and crème brûleé, drinking a tall cold glass of lemonade after walking through the Sahara, drinking a malted milkshake after walking through the Sahara, whatever it is you want to drink after walking through the Sahara, diving into a swimming pool."

"You said you've never been to Europe, Gloria Girl. Can I also assume you've never traversed the Sahara?"

"Yeah but I can assume. It was all the experiences. It was a Slim Aarons photo, a ride in a race car, the first time seeing the Pacific Ocean, the Redwood Forest, the Gulf Stream waters, Amber waves of grain and seeing the Beatles on Ed Sullivan and then hearing the radio announcer declare that World War was over. And watching Mahalia Jackson sing the Star-Spangled Banner."

"Jesus girl. Is it just because he's famous? He can't be that hot."

"He's that hot. But it's not just how he looks. It's the way he moves and the way he points at things and the way he looks at you and the way his curls bounce and the whole thing."

"Impossible."

"You haven't seen him."

"I've seen guys who were perfect. And none of them did that to me."

"This one would. He does to me."

So when a guy can make an ordinary Tuesday in October 1982 feel like that...she, almost inadvertently, quasi instinctively, definitely intentionally but definitely with an element of involuntariness also, touched his left arm. It was positioned on the desk to her immediate left as he leaned over her to read the microfiche screen. His thumb was magnificent. There was a torn and muddy cuff of a rugby shirt over a highly scratched and highly dinged Cartier watch and there between the muddy rugby shirt cuff and tattered leather watch strap was his arm hair and wrist and sinew and skin. She touched it; more like she was compelled to touch it; or she couldn't not touch it. Or she couldn't have not touched it. And her fingers lingered for an extra beat.

After while her fingers were still firmly on his wrist, and actually moving back and forth ever so slightly, almost imperceptibly she had this moment when she said to herself, "I am touching JFK Junior's arm."

In high school, she had a friend whose house backed up to a prison. One night this friend had a sleepover and they stole some peach schnapps from the parents and drank some and then decided to go touch the prison walls. They all just ran outside, ran through her backyard, ran over some fields, and touched the wall of the prison. That was it. But it was invigorating to do something forbidden, to not only be in such proximity to something so dangerous, but to come into physical contact with it. It was the same feeling people get when they go see Niagara Falls; or go to Graceland and feel something Elvis once wore. It was like that. Again, Gloria had to assume as she had never been to Graceland. She just wanted to touch JFK Junior's arm.

While her fingers lingered on his arm she looked up and behind her and directly at John who was simultaneously bewildered and intrigued. Neither one of them said anything. She let go of his arm then stood up slowly, turned around, and kissed him. He kissed back and they started to make out after a few minutes of which she felt his erection and started to giggle. Another giggle, neither coy nor submissive but not as sophisticated and self-assured as the giggle with which she greeted him; this one more silly and carefree. John laughed too. She said, through stifled giggles, "I can feel your Horace Mann-hood." He laughed too.

They fucked right there on the microfiche machine.

Viscosity

There is a certain ease that comes from following directions; a certain tranquility that comes from doing as you are told; a certain lubrication to a life done doing what is expected of you. Both Gloria and John knew this. They were both people who avoided friction. They had both played the sports, gone to the schools, gone to the churches, went to the parties, worn the clothes, made the friends, taken the jobs, and gone to the places they were told.

So this was less surprising than some might think.

Gloria had merely tasted independence. She hadn't even chosen her own college (not really as geography and costs had been such enormous factors in her decision) so moving to a new city was really the first thing she had done that was *hers*. She enjoyed it. She was enjoying it. With respect to love, she had dated a football player in high school and a frat boy in college, neither of whom inspired nor were inspiring when it came to all of that, the risks and the yearning and the inability to focus on anything else but the small patch of real estate between cuff and watch band. Her prison wall adventure notwithstanding, Gloria had never really done much too daring. Touching John's arm was in part, a way to remedy that.

Similarly, John had never had the opportunity to wonder what he might want to do before he could ever decide not to do it. He had no idea who he was; who he might want to be. On top of all that, being JFK Jr. was not fun. It was hard to even masturbate when you're JFK Jr., not because he didn't love himself, he did, but because he to make sure no one could walk in on him in his bedroom or bathroom and the bathroom in his apartment in an old Providence brownstone had no lock. Who wouldn't snap a Polaroid of JFK Jr. jerking off for a million bucks? And that was before you even got another person involved. Dating was not easy either; actually dating and acquiring the girl was a cinch; trusting her was not. He always had everything to lose with every move he made.

And while the door on the mixed media room in the basement of the archives did not lock either, you could turn off the lights and put the sign that said, "Making Library Rounds. Be Back in 15 minutes." And no one would bother you.

So this – this thing that was part dare and part functional equivalent to masturbation and part declaration of independence and part brief fling where theyboth have something to lose and therefore these potential losses sort of cancel themselves out – was just fun. Two people who without even realizing it had been yearning to say "Fuck it. I want to do it my way" for years and finally had the courage and the opportunity to do so.

Do Me Decimal System

Over the next six weeks they had sex with some frequency; like ten times maybe? Neither was counting. Each night or two per week that she worked nights. It was a sacrifice, an initiation of sorts to make the new people work until midnight. And she got paid extra. And she didn't have anything to do after work anyway so she might as well work nights and screw JFK Jr., she figured. She could have done more things to her apartment like hung up artwork or joined some local clubs or gotten a library card or done some volunteering or recaulk her bathtub; but why clean your bathroom when you can have sex with JFK Jr.?

And there would be time for all that apartment stuff she figured.

She slept with her boyfriend in high school – awkward times in the back of his car - and the boy in college. But this was on another level. This was daring. And grown up. There could be, in addition to the biological and emotional consequences, professional ones as well. It was irresponsible, cavalier, foolhardy, fun. It was a declaration of independence. She knew it wasn't love. It was more like cocaine. He was a jolt that made her feel good. That made her feel alive. He was intoxicating and forbidden and illegal and elusive and addictive and enticing and something she knew she would never bring home to mother. She had feelings but they were evanescent and transient. Like the feelings that come from cocaine.

And like her Paris and Graceland analogies, Gloria had to concede that she had never done cocaine. But he was what she imagined cocaine would be like.

"This is fun." She said to him once.

"It is. Thank you."

"Thank you."

"When I was a kid," he began, "we learned about how to find things in the card catalog and the Dewey decimal system and all that. I don't think those librarians prepared me for this."

"Yeah well in library school we learned how to pick out the most fuckable library patrons. We called it the Do Me Decimal System."

"Really?"

"No John. Not really. There was no Do Me Decimal System. There is no Do Me Decimal System."

"Pardon my naivete." He laughed.

"You think you're naïve?" she asked, intrigued by this conversation. (They had spoken before. About Horace Mann and Horace Mann's educative policies; and about what they liked in terms of nibbling on ears and so forth during the act; and comments on each other's bodies; and the general state of things, i.e., "I have so much laundry to do and no quarters," "Those socks look really comfortable," "The chocolate milk at the Ratty is so good but it can't be good for you," "My mom would be so mad if she knew I wore these socks to play rugby.")

"Yeah. I've been pretty sheltered."

"I remember seeing you in my grandma's Life magazine when your mom married that Greek shipping tycoon."

"That's not real life, GW." (He called her GW.)

"It's not sheltered."

"It's way sheltered. Maybe sheltered isn't the right word."

"What's the right word?"

"Inauthentic. That's the right word. The way I grew up was inauthentic."

"You resent that?"

"Sometimes."

"You don't seem resentful. Or angry. You're actually pretty fun. And funny."

"Thanks, GW."

"You think of George Washington when we screw, don't you?"

"Not at all." He replied. Before pausing, "Well maybe once or twice. Also that rhymes."

She laughed. How could she not laugh. He was so fun.

He finished tying his shoes, his nasty rugby cleats which most women would have licked if given the opportunity to do so, put his backpack over his shoulder, grabbed the stack of Horace Mann papers she had located and printed for him, playfully patted her shoulder, opened the archives room door, playfully looked both ways, then very histrionically made his exit.

She knew that one of these days, a day which was likely imminent, would be the last day she ever saw him do that.

Girl Talk

The time she told Ruth she was having sex with JFK Jr. was a very fun night. It was a Saturday in November and they were in her apartment drinking wine and she just told her, the same way you would tell someone that you had enjoyed a Caesar Salad for lunch.

"JFK Jr. and I are having sex."

"Bullshit," she said, mouth agape.

"I swear."

"Bullshit," she repeated, mouth still agape while pushing Gloria in the shoulder playfully.

"You made me spill my wine."

"Then stop lying to me."

"I'm not lying."

"You want me to believe that you and John Fitzgerald Kennedy, Jr., the guy with the minty cardamom breath, are fucking."

"Am I that ugly?" They erupted into a giggle. "Am I that fucking ugly that it is so hard for you to believe that JFK Jr. would want to have sex with me?"

They then spent the next ninety minutes like this. Refilling their wine glasses and giggling as Gloria described what had been going on for the last couple weeks; giggling as Ruth asked her all about his appendages and his smells and his techniques and his sounds and then asking for more details, "exactly *how* big" and "so it is more of a grunt or more of a sigh or more of a moan" and Gloria, finally able to talk to someone about the last few weeks, answered all her questions about his appendages and his smells and his techniques and his sounds and tolerated Ruth's need for more specificity when it came to clarifying and distinguishing between a groan and a grunt and a sigh or a wheeze. Gloria told her all about the layout of the basement archives room, the machinery and mechanisms upon which they screwed, how screwing on her boss's office chair was rather gratifying, the way he could be shy and forceful at the same time, the way he could make her cum several times.

At the end of the conversation Ruth asked, "This doesn't end well, does it?" And Gloria shook her head "No" and then cried until Ruth started laughing again letting Gloria know it was ok to laugh.

A Good Place to Be Somebody

When he went to inter-fraternity formals, John's neckties were always askew and his blazers often missing a button and he would often wear a dirty baseball cap, all of this to put people at ease but a little to make his own declaration of independence. He would not take himself or any of the things that came with being *him* too seriously. He wore mismatched socks and scarves and pajama tops to class. He loved Brown as he got four free years to try things, try things out, try out who he wanted to be. He played Frisbee and rugby with fraternity brothers. He ate in the cafeteria and marveled at the rejuvenating coldness of the chocolate milk on those rare instances when he was hung over and he waited in line for the ice cream. He handed in papers, papers frequently stained by cffee mugs and smudged correction fluid marks and with the perforated dotted edges of dot matrix printer paper still attached, at the last possible hour. When he failed to pay parking tickets, his car was towed. When he was short of change, he scrounged for coffee money. He did not carry money around with him. He was academically inquisitive and both cognizant and intolerant of injustices – social, economic. He wore jeans and Hawaiian shirts and he liked the cafeteria pizza and students nudged one another in the ribs when they saw him. He lived in a dorm his freshman year and then the Phi Kappa Psi fraternity house and then an apartment on Benefit Street where he had four roommates. He was refined but still easygoing; he was intrinsically graceful but not afraid – perhaps even eager – to be clumsy; and despite his awareness of all of the artifice in the world, he projected an air of genuineness. When meeting someone, he always introduced himself, never taking for granted that nearly everyone alive already knew who he was.

But this celebrity from which he almost intrinsically recoiled was inescapable. Visitors to campus sought directions to his dorm room. Photographers often snuck onto campus to catch a picture of him. He had parts in campus productions of plays such as *How to Succeed in Business Without Really Trying* and *No Place to Be Somebody*. Although he had some talent and the right charisma for acting, he never seriously considered it as a career. On closing night, he had a cast party at his apartment. His apartment was decorated - things matched, there were tasteful furnishings and appointments – but he also had dust bunnies and a clanking radiator and piles of dirty laundry in his room. People drank too much and smoked and he got to drink too much and smoke and forget that he was America's prince for a few hours. For one production, he was asked to cut his hair. He got a crew cut and was elated when he realized that people no longer recognized him when he walked into bars.

He loved his sister and was so proud when she came to one of his plays. During the end of the first act, when the actors backstage heard an exceptionally exuberant laugh from the audience, singular and confident and warm, John leaned over and whispered, "That's my sister. That's Caroline."

Through it all, he retained his sense of humor.

He hadn't slept with that many women. Certainly less than one would think. His mother had impressed upon him how parasitic people could be, the responsibility he had to his legacy, his name, how easy it would be to mess everything up, how publicly and how shamefully such a failure would be. He liked Gloria. Liked their chats nearly as much as he liked their sexual encounters. Liked the necessary discretion she afforded, how she would be in lots of trouble if she told anyone about him and them. This fostered some genuine communication, he could share with her the things he wanted, expected, hoped for, most of which, to put it succinctly, he didn't know. How would a 22-year-old kid know all this? His political science professors would ask him if he wanted to enter politics and he would say something charming like, "No. My mother would kill me." And the professors would laugh and wonder if he was being ironic in light of the assassination or assassinations plural. He liked acting but would he ever be able to escape his persona?

Likely not. What did he want to do? What did he have a responsibility to do?

He loved Diana Ross's "It's My Turn;" he loved Juice Newton and Air Supply, he also loved Stevie Wonder and Rush and Elvis Costello; he wanted to like the Violent Femmes, because one of his frat brothers' dad was a music producer and responsible for signing the band and people went nuts when they heard them at parties, but just somehow couldn't; he wanted to like Bloody Marys because he liked the idea of drinks with a celery in it but just couldn't stomach the tomato juice; he wasn't a big drinker, he got drunk in college now and again but drunkenness meant letting your guard down and that was a luxury he could not oft-afford; and you only had to see Uncle Teddy fall down the stairs a few times before you came to suspect that alcohol was not always fun as it looked. He loved the baked scrod at the Ratty; he loved talking with Fatima, the Portuguese woman who checked ID cards at the Ratty.

Driving In Your Car I Never Never Want to Go Home

One night they went for a drive. They walked to her apartment and she drove them both in the Oldsmobile Omega. They drove for hours and just meandered about the small state of Rhode Island. They talked about ordinary things like the best pizza and mud stains and music and they listened to the radio and she was touched by how he yearned to talk. "What a wonderful world this is" he said. "Providence?" she asked. "No this car. No pings or scanners or facial recognition devices and no way for anyone to find us and Sheena Easton playing on the radio." She looked at him then, his profile against the night sky, the light from the streetlights bouncing and frolicking about the car.

Goodbye, Margaret Thatcher

She knew there was a code to this sort of thing – the affair, such an adult word - an adult code of which she was unaware because you quite necessarily can only learn about standards of adult behavior by being and adult and engaging in adult behaviors.

John stopped by Gloria's desk once after Thanksgiving break. And she could tell as soon as he rounded the corner that there would be no more fun, no more sex, no more adventure. This was her first foray into this world; these worlds; she was a visitor on so many fronts, to both the Ivy League world and the adult world. She suspected this sort of thing happened all the time. They called it casual sex for a reason, didn't they? So she decided to be casual. They shook hands and she told him that it was nice meeting him. She actually said, "It was very nice to have met you." The same thing one might have said after meeting then-Secretary of State George Schultz or then-Prime Minister Margaret Thatcher.

There was no proscribed etiquette for these sorts of things and a finite number of possible things to say:

"Nice to have met you."

"It was nice meeting you."

"Hey thanks for the laughs."

Later, when she got sad about things – and she often did – she would think mostly about their goodbye. How she thanked him and shook his hand and gave him a terse and polite farewell when what she really wanted to do is…. Is what? She had no idea what she might have done differently. She knew the rules, i.e., there were no rules, to this when she first grabbed his ass as he was peering over some letter Horace Mann penned to someone one hundred fifty years ago. The fact she even knew who Horace Mann was sort of pissed her off. But she wasn't really pissed off was she?

She had fun too.

It was fun. At the same time though it was also a loss. Even though the post-JFK Jr. status quo felt much like resuming the pre-JFK Jr. status quo, something still felt different; somehow felt lessened; diminished. It was the loss of something more that the status quo even though she knew that he was borrowing her and that she was borrowing him and she knew that he knew that she was borrowing him and he knew that she knew that he was merely borrowing her. That's all any relationship is anyway right? You merely borrow that person for a while. The while is sometimes minutes and sometimes weeks and sometimes decades. This was how she was able to tell herself that he was not discarding her. Leaving her. She was never his. Of course they had never discussed this, never named or labeled their relationship or discussed if it even rose to the level of a relationship. And nothing he ever said or did or didn't say or didn't do indicated he didn't appreciate her. It was just something that Gloria instinctively knew. Like the way you just know a grandparent loves you. Grandparents never really say they love you because that is just not the way that grandparents are, but they do. And you know it. It's also possible to know that someone doesn't love you and never will.

So yeah, Tuesday after Thanksgiving break John walked to the desk and just looked at her with a smile that was sort of more a smirk and he put his elbows on the desk and his chin in his hands and he said, "I'm just about all done with Horace Mann."

"Which means we're both done with the Horace Mannhood thing."

"I guess so."

Then they high fived and Gloria said, "good job" and then they shook hands and that's when Gloria said, "It was nice to have met you."

And that is the very last time she ever saw him. Though she thought she might have seen him once that following Spring when she was walking somewhere for lunch and she saw the back of a head covered with curly black hair and a backpack like the kind he had. And she was surprised by how little she felt.

Though the majority of her feelings then were feelings related to morning sickness and bloating.

Gary M. Almeter

Commencement

John Kennedy graduated from Brown University in June 1983, without knowing that the hot librarian in the basement of the John Hay Library was carrying his baby. That day the Secret Service men fanned out across the grounds. Jackie arrived. People snapped her picture. She smiled. There were crowds. Providence sweltered. Most everyone had a wicked hangover. They'd loved, partied, danced, studied, and soon they'd be a bunch of kids who were supposed to be adults but were really kids who go do other kid things in other big places.

In this way, John Kennedy Jr.'s public life was launched.

Graduation day, Gloria woke up early, put on a loose-fitting though decidedly non-maternity sundress and running shoes and went for a walk. Her first June in Providence and the sun was barely up. The campus, always nearly perfectly manicured, was both perfectly manicured – the lawns and the azaleas and forsythia and barrels of tulips and geraniums and window boxes of alstroemeria to make it seem as though the good Lord himself had just mowed and trimmed and pruned each - and thoroughly adorned with brown and maroon flags and banners and bunting all splayed perfectly and each adorned with the Brown University crest, its red cross between four open books underneath a radiant half-sun.

Gloria was nearly seven months pregnant and pretending she wasn't. She hadn't told her family. And wouldn't. She hadn't told her employer. And wouldn't. She hadn't told the baby's father and wouldn't. For three reasons. First, she couldn't tell him. She had never known his phone number.

They had never exchanged such information. She had never asked him for his numbers or addresses. He was graduating that day and soon she would have no idea where he was or how to reach him. He mentioned growing up on Fifth Avenue once while getting dressed. That was about all she knew. She had been to New York City once as a kid. Second, she wouldn't tell him even if she could. He didn't want to be a father yet and she wasn't prepared to alter the course of history. How could she be the one to do *that* to John Fitzgerald Kennedy, Jr.? Lastly, she did not want to be an asterisk or footnote in the Kennedy history, her only legacy being what was done to her by a more-famous man. She did not want to relinquish control of her life.

Perhaps someone in the admissions office or alumnbi relations office could have told her what his address was. But she had not known anyone there.

Her obstetrician knew she was pregnant and did not blink when Gloria told her that she did nogt know who the father was. ("Everything looks great!") She didn't have to tell Ruth because Ruth was with her in her apartment in January when she took her pregnancy test.

Gloria donned a baggy sundress and went for a walk on graduation morning and as she did the graduates began to emerge – from brownstones, from dorms, from large apartment buildings off campus, from houses converted to student living to begin the first day of the rest of their lives. There was a general aura of disorientation on the streets – parents trying to find the diners and cafes at which they were told to meet their graduates; graduates hung over and reluctant to leave the comfort and safety of Brown, reluctant to leave the boyfriends and girlfriends with whom they had just spent one last night, reluctant to leave the sororities and fraternities and manicured lawns and all you can eat meals in the cafeterias and impromptu Frisbee on the quad and impromptu lacrosse and impromptu hacky sack and impromptu parties and porches. This day was to be – like most of life would be for the Brown University Class of 1983 – perfectly choreographed with breakfast with parents and then a meeting at the quad and the march into commencement and the speakers and then the procession out and then the dinner with family and then the trip to wherever they would go next: medical School, law school, graduate school, Boston, New York, Washington, Madison Avenue, Wall Street, Hong Kong, London, Tokyo, Frankfurt, Paris.

Gloria knew that his family would be here. Everyone did. As she walked she wondered if they went to breakfast before commencement. If they had reservations at one of Providence's Italian restaurants that evening. If they needed reservations or if Jackie could just walk into any restaurant and be served immediately. Or if they would be going back to New York City promptly. For meetings. Or better restaurants. She wondered what their "family dynamic" was like.

They hadn't talked at great length about his mother or his father. But he had told her during a post-coital conversation that his mother would surprise people – she was fun and surprisingly tolerant of things for which people would not expect her to be tolerant and that while she was determined to teach her son about the world she also gave him wide berth to be who he was. So she pictured her entering her son's apartment that morning and seeing the beer cans and the ash trays and the socks and the bags of chips and the notebooks strewn about the living room and being nonchalant about the mess.

She wondered if she blended in as she walked – if all the parents and siblings of graduates merely assumed that she was graduating too and on her way to meet her own parents and she was nursing her own hangover and would soon be walking across stage to pick up her diploma and soon thereafter begin a career in medicine or engineering or law or heading to London or Hong Kong to do whatever one does in Hong Kong and London. Did they have reason to think she was not a Brown student? That she wasn't Ivy League material? It had only been one year since she graduated from Syracuse and while the year since had been momentous in many respects, it could not have aged her *that* much. Then she realized that these people, particularly on a day such as this, are not the sort of people to wonder about others, especially on a day like today. She was the only one who knew how anomalous she was and what was growing in her belly and whose it was.

She did not see him. Nor did she think she would. Nor did she want to. Though she secretly did want to.

Independence Day

A few weeks later, she and Ruth drove to Newport where they could sit on a beach and Gloria could wear a bathing suit without anyone from work spotting her and her belly. Ruth brought a picnic lunch. She made watercress sandwiches. They talked about their plan for when they give birth. And by they, they meant Gloria all by herself.

"I am nearly certain that I'll be able to get you in and out of the hospital undetected. It's just a matter of entering through the ER and then creating enough chaos so that I can sneak you out once you have the baby."

"Sounds fun."

"Yeah. It'll be a blast. We'll use a fake name and by the time the insurance and billing people get all their shit together you'll be gone."

"Are you going to get in trouble?"

"I better not. I hope not. I'm not expecting to. Just look confused and terrified and like you might go bonkers if anyone asks you for any specifics."

"I can do that. I do that every day."

"I have a few more Ts to cross and a few more Is to dot but I think it's possible."

"Does that mean I can't get drugs?"

"I'm working on it Glor."

"I'd love some drugs."

"I know babe."

"It hurts doesn't it?"

"Yes babe."

They nibble on watercress.

"Thank you, Ruth."

"I should be the one thanking you for the adventure of a lifetime."

"Is sneaking a woman into a hospital by manufacturing her identity and then sneaking her and her new baby out of the hospital a few hours later unethical?"

"Probably. However, it's definitely less unethical than a university librarian sleeping with a student at the university."

"We are both so good at being unethical. Does this university know how goddamn lucky they are that we are here?"

"One can hope, Glor."

"It's not like I was his professor. And it's not like he was in 7th grade or something. Do nurses have to take the Hippocratic oath."

"We don't. I took the Nightingale pledge at graduation. Besides there's nothing in the Hippocratic oath specifically about not doing this."

"Good. I feel better already."

"Good."

"Pass me that suntan oil."

On the drive home, Gloria driving the Oldsmobile Omega with the windows open, Ruth asked, "You sure you want to give the baby up for adoption?"

"Yes. Definitely. I just can't…My parents just couldn't…"

"I understand."

"Can we just leave him or her on the steps of a convent somewhere?"

"I'll look into it."

"That means if he or she ever wants to find me he or she likely won't be able to. I think I'm ok with that."

"Honey you don't worry about three decades from now you worry about today. Then tomorrow you worry about tomorrow. OK?"

"Got it."

"Good."

"Thanks Ruth."

"Anytime."

"Anytime? You mean you would do this again?"

"Of course," Ruth responded.

"Hopefully this is the last time we do this."

Their Milieu

There were times she imagined all of this happening under different circumstances. She'd be married to a millionaire; like in a Slim Aarons photo. She'd be poolside in an audacious caftan or on a chairlift with a fur-lined hoodie perfectly circumnavigating her face or on a beach fearlessly in a midriff-baring terry cloth pant suit.

Ready to Pop

She spoke with her parents regularly, they always called her so she would not have to pay for the call. One day Gloria's mother asked her how she was doing and, forgetting she was speaking with her mother or forgetting it was all supposed to be a secret or maybe secretly yearning to tell the people she loved most and who loved her best about the only thing she thought about, said, "I feel huge and am ready to pop." Concerned, her mother asked, "Have you not been eating right?" The Gloria snapped back to and made something up about going to an Italian restaurant and eating too much pasta. But then Gloria had to get off the phone immediately as she was on the cusp of starting to cry. For a number of reasons.

Birth Day / September 12, 1983

Gloria was someone's mother for approximately thirty-six hours, though her sense of time was sort of messed up for that week. She and Ruth dropped a healthy 8-pound, day-and-a-half old baby boy on the steps of an orphanage in Fall River, MA. They put him in a basket and everything. They left the basket (and the baby) on the steps of a place called "Orphelinat St. Joseph", the literal translation of which from the French means "St. Joseph's Orphanage," a place Ruth identified and researched. Gloria didn't think orphanages like this one really existed in real life. Or had ever existed outside of movies about witches and vampires – large, imposing, multi-storied, Gothic-looking structures, had there been gargoyles affixed to ledge where the obscenely sloped roof met the façade, Gloria would not have been surprised. And while Ruth assured her that the nuns who dwelled within its walls were good nuns, or at least nuns with a good reputation, Gloria had been unable to formulate any thoughts on the place; was neither thinking nor capable of cogent thought during this time, a day and a half after birthing her son.

Ruth, with an armload of stolen blankets, snuck Gloria out of the hospital the evening of the 14th and into Ruth's car - a white Datsun 510 – as Gloria was still on painkillers. Gloria held the boy and the basket on her lap in the basket as they drove the quick trip up I-95 to Fall River.

They drove in silence; Gloria rested her head against the window of the Datsun. The streetlights intermittently illuminated his little baby face so every other second or so was spent observing him in similarly intermittent fashion. He was resting and cooing in what she could only assume was comfort. Was this the very first time she had ever held a baby? It might be. She couldn't recall a time when she had held one before.

"Almost there." Ruth said.

"You can drive as slow as you want."

"Anything you need? Tell me what you need."

"I'm fine I think."

"You're doing the right thing."

And Gloria just wept.

They arrived at the orphanage. Gloria kissed her son on the forehead, rubbed his little cheek, kissed him on the forehead again, and then handed the basket that held him to Ruth. Ruth got out, scurried up the large stone steps, set him down, pounded on the door with her fist, then ran down the steps and back into the running car. They waited for a nun to open the door and find the basket before they drove away. Ruth had smeared mud on her license plates so none of the nuns could write down her plate numbers. The nun who opened the door did look perfectly nice. Though women of Gloria and Ruth's age had learned, as his trials and arrest and perpetual malfeasance wended their way through the news cycle, from Ted Bundy that even good looking people could be monsters. Was this nun a cannibal? Nothing they could do about it now. They drove away and back to Gloria's apartment, Ruth stayed with her and they ordered pizza and watched *Magnum, P.I.* and *Knot's Landing* as Ruth gave Gloria sitz-baths, administered the stolen painkillers, and generally took care of her.

It was easy to steal painkillers in the 1980s.

A decade or so later, there'd be a high-profile criminal case where a teen mother allegedly gave birth at the prom, discarded the baby in a bathroom garbage can, and then proceeded back to the prom. People would be shocked by this.

Gloria would not be shocked by this. She would understand completely how such a thing might happen.

When does a woman even become a mother? Maybe a woman becomes a mother when a baby emerges from her womb and from that point on she can never stop being a mother no matter how much or how little mothering she actually does. Maybe a woman becomes a mother as soon as a spermatozoa fertilizes her ovum. Theologians and scientists and Caucasian men in Congress all differ on that front. If a turtle lays some eggs in the sand somewhere and then swims off and never returns, the turtle will still be a mother turtle if the eggs she laid in the sand hatch. She won't even be cognizant of her motherhood, but a mother she will be. But maybe it's different for humans what with the sophistication and intellect and complex machinery and complex ways of thinking.

Gloria Winegar's motherhood was more ... nebulous. There were no documents identifying her as such; she had provided the hospital doctors with a false name and Ruth had been switching and swapping and doctoring all the clipboards that hung on her bed. In that first few days, she would wonder if she would always be a mother. A child she had birthed was *somewhere,* and while that *somewhere* was *elsewhere* the boy existed. He was a boy. With a whole life to lead; a whole wild and unpredictable life. But even though he existed, he was separate and apart from her and neither cognizant of the fact he existed nor of the concept of "mother." Or family. Or loyalty. Or guilt. Or biology. Or how a woman can try to do what's best and be certain that she has done what is best and still feel the sort of rotten that makes her feel like she will never ever ever feel good again. Which is how Gloria felt, like she would never ever feel good again; that it would be a metaphysical impossibility for her to ever feel anything but shame and sadness ever again. Ruth told her it was the hormones and the drugs.

Ruth. Goddamn Ruth. There would be a place in heaven for Ruth. Assuming the nuns hadn't seen her and cursed her with a nun spell. In and out of sleep, she dreamt the nuns at the Fall River orphanage were conduits for child labor slave trade with the drug cartel and they sold the babies to Central America so that the drug cartel could use the babies to harvest the poppies that make their heroin. Or maybe they sold her baby to a fishing boat captain who made her baby spend his youth hauling in big nets of fish and he was so scared by the fish guts the men chopping off the fish heads with big oddly shaped rusty knives designed solely for chopping off fish heads and who glared and sneered at him if he looked at them; he'd be tasked with peeling off all the fish skin with another oddly shaped rusty knife. It would smell and the men curse and be smelly and her poor baby boy would not know any better because it is the only life he would ever know because the nuns – well they need to survive too so in those instances when someone left a baby in a basket on their doorstep (which were far more common than she realized she told herself; it happened practically every day she told herself) had to sell him to the highest bidder and like any black market operation like the sale of organs and human trafficking the highest bidder is more often than not someone with nefarious intentions.

"I'm sorry about all this little man," she moaned.

Some mothers do not want to be with their children. But there are degrees of this. Some mothers never ever want to be with their children and thusly, give those children away. Some mothers will never ever think about those children again. Perhaps necessarily. Perhaps out of some sort of apathy. Some mothers will think about the children they give away every single day for the rest of their lives. Some mothers might experience episodes of not wanting to be with their children. Like on days when it is raining or when it snows so hard that school is closed and the children are stuck inside and they are fighting with their siblings and complaining about how they have nothing to do and do not want to eat what the mother just made for dinner and then they will go outside to play in the snow and it will take thirty minutes to bundle them up and they will be back in the house in eight minutes and leave snow and boots and craves and mittens all over the house. Or when the child breaks a vase with a football. Or a window. A mother will wish she were not there. Or maybe later on when a child tells its mother he or she is gay and the mother is a conservative and intolerant Christian and the mother will disown the child. Sometimes a daughter will be pregnant or marrying someone of whom the mother disapproves. Surely on any given day mothers will wish their children were sleeping and wish that while those children slept they could be on a beach somewhere themselves drinking pina coladas. Some mothers do not want to become mothers but excel at motherhood nonetheless. Some mothers want to be with their children but understand that the children will better off someplace else. And with someone else.

The next few days were like this; Gloria, in addition to the pain and bleeding and lactation suppression, felt like she would never be normal again, like she was standing in a foot of water in a cold basement from which she would never be allowed to leave. Her mind raced:

What happens next? Nothing she guessed. She'd go back to work. Try to be ordinary. Try to be regular. Try not to get into trouble. Try not to break down. Would she ever meet him? Would she ever feel human again? What had she just done? Is this how life is going to be for her from now on – a state of perpetual wonder about what her son was doing and where he was doing it?

Though surely parents who keep their children (what are parents who keep their children called? For brevity's sake she would refer to them as "parents") surely ask themselves "what have we just done to ourselves?" when they bring home their babies. Life as they know it changes for them also. She was neither unique nor deserving of much sympathy. And would find a way to deal.

Hunting Cap

She imagined that, years later, her baby boy would hear stories of babies left on doorsteps in baskets and think it impossible for it to ever happen in real life. Maybe he'd be watching a movie with his parents or parent and in the movie the nun or the fireman or the whoever would open the door and say "Oh my goodness! What do we have here?" He'd laugh and ask, "Mommy is that where babies come from?" and his mom will have to make a quick decision about what to say. Maybe he'd know about his adoption already. Maybe he wouldn't have a mom. Maybe he would have two dads. Or one dad.

In an odd way, Gloria knew she was lucky. Because she happened to get pregnant after befriending a woman at new employee orientation at Brown University who ended up being an obstetrics nurse at Women & Infants Hospital about 10 minutes from the apartment.

What a year it had been.

She had to assume that the nuns at Orphelinat St. Joseph were good nuns. That this happened to them all the time and they knew just what to do. That they had a network of parish priests who they would call whenever a baby arrived on their steps and the priests knew just what to do to connect that baby with loving parents in their parish. She had to assume that this happened to Catholics with some frequency – what with the repression and the shame and the disdain – so the nuns sprung into action every time they heard a cry at their door. They had a long list of parents – good Catholic husbands and wives who had tried and tried to have babies but could not – parents who had suffered miscarriages and years of monthly disappointments who then went to their local parish priest and asked him what to do. The priest inevitably had a clipboard hanging somewhere near his desk, with mimeographed pages with spaces for names and addresses and phone numbers and probably contact information for three references and the parents wrote their names down on the paper and handed the clipboard back to the priest who gave everything a perfunctory look over to make sure it was ok and then encouraged the parents to make a donation because moving babies was not easy nor was it cheap and God looked favorably upon those who helped Him do his work. Then the priest sent this paper to the nun orphanages who had their own clipboards and when a baby arrived they called the priest and he arranged everything. This, she told herself, all happened smoothly and flawless to and for her baby boy.

She told herself that he was resting in a long-dormant nursery in the home of a couple who had been yearning for a baby. They moved quickly, those nuns. They walked slowly but they moved quickly when it came to abandoned infants. Their whole job – the whole reason they exist – was to take care of people and she was certain they took care of him.

And one day they would be watching that movie about babies on nun doorsteps with his mom and his dad and likely a brother and sister because the parents would love him so much and be so astonished at how *easy* he was *how good he was* that would want to no *need* to adopt more babies. And those parents would wonder if they had a finite amount of love and if that love is divisible and how could they give but a fraction of their love to him, their first adopted baby but then a wise person would tell them that love multiplies.

Or maybe a gruff great aunt would – through her cigarette smoke – say something gruff about how she didn't have time to worry about love because she was working at O'Malley's Pub three nights a week because her husband had been a drunk bastard who worked on the docks and spent his pay check, what a pittance it was, at McDooley's Irish Pub and they had seven children and no one ever asked her one goddamned thing about love. No. That wouldn't happen.

No. His parents would love him. They would not be wealthy. But they would love him. Only blue-collar people would go to a priest for a baby – wealthy people would hire a surrogate or pay someone at Harvard for a test tube of their semen and eggs to make the baby because how could you not? If given the choice? Or maybe they would get the eggs of a Harvard lady professor and the semen of Larry Bird or John McEnroe or Lawrence Taylor.

Or maybe once his mom and dad (is that what he would call them or would he call them Pops and Moms or something?) had a baby they could exhale and relax a little bit and not worry about eggs and fertilization angles and spermatozoa and they would make their own babies and he would worry that they love the baby they made more than his own self who wasn't even really theirs but soon his gears would be assuaged because he would always be their first and they waited way longer than nine months for him and they wanted him so badly and the day that priest called them with the news of a baby at some orphanage in Fall River was the happiest day of their whole lives.

Would he know he was adopted? Would he have found some secret documents while hunting for Christmas presents? Would his dad have Playboy magazines hidden in his bedroom? Would they be smokers? Drinkers? Singers? Musicians? Do they work bingo at this church? Would Father McWhomever make them work bingo to say thank you for the adoption? Would they have pets? A swimming pool? Would they play tennis? Backgammon? Chess? Golf? Hockey? Are they in Boston? A suburb? Would his parents live on one of the floors of a triple decker? Or would he be somewhere south of the city – where his parents would be reliant on the sea for their survival? Or might these nuns function all over New England? Could he be in Maine? New Hampshire? Would he live in the woods? In a cabin? Would everything he ate be slathered in maple syrup? Would he chop wood to keep his house warm? Would he wear black and red wool hunting caps? Like Holden Caulfield? What would they name him? Would his name be Holden?

Sister Leonella

Sister Leonella was reading in the first-floor library of the orphanage on the evening of September 14, 1983. She, younger and newer than her housemates, stayed up later. She saw headlights drive down St. Joseph Street, which was a little unusual given the late hour but nothing to warrant concern. Then she heard some knocking on the front door. When she went to the front door she found a new baby in a basket and saw a small car drive away.

She had heard the other sisters talk about how this used to happen, still might happen, but used to happen with some frequency. There were no protocols in place for when it happened, no forms in triplicate in a tray on the credenza by the door to get filled out immediately, no one on staff to handle it.

She took the baby out of the basket and unwrapped the blanket and looked him over. He looked healthy, ten fingers and ten toes, and said to herself that he was about to make someone very very happy. She just held the baby for a while. She was an aunt and had held her siblings' kids pretty regularly when they were brand new. And liked them. Liked it. Holding babies. She held him for a little bit longer then decided it was time to wake up Sister Helena, the head nun. Sister Helena took over from there.

Sister Leonella gathered the basket and blanket and put it in her storage unit in the basement.

Back to Work

Gloria went back to work six days after she gave birth. Missing days so early in the semester was a big no-no. She was able to manufacture a flu to call in sick and explain a noticeable weight loss. To explain a two and a half hour visit to the bathroom, she told her boss that she had a meeting with a Classics professor. It was odd working with people who had no idea that something momentous had happened in her life. She liked her colleagues. But there was just no way she could have started the job a mere year ago, and then three months into it, told them she was pregnant. With a Brown student's baby.

She had been able to hide her pregnancy the whole time. She was tall and her elongated torso kept her from showing. That is what Ruth told her; even used the term "elongated torso." Ruth told her that the pregnancies of tall women – especially those who have elongated torsos – do not show. Ruth was a nurse. She knew this stuff. So because of her absurdly long torso, she was able to wear big flowy sweaters and big flowy blouses and long flowy sundresses and no one ever knew she was pregnant. His September arrival was perfectly timed so she could wear long flowy sundresses – the most effective means of camouflage – when she was at her largest. Which still wasn't very big. Given her elongated torso.

Her mind wandered. She figured her baby boy would be tall. John was tall. She was tall. Ruth said that he was long when he was born. 23.5 inches. Which meant nothing to Gloria. Presumably he was still long; at the age of six days. What did he look like? Who would he look like? She spent another twenty minutes in the bathroom at work crying. Ruth said this would happen. "They call it post-partum depression for a reason," she told Gloria.

Gloria missed her mom. She hadn't been back to Homer since Christmas as family would have known she was pregnant. She felt guilty for all the lies she had told her parents; all the conferences she had manufactured whenever they threw out dates they could come see her; whenever they called her on their dime. She felt guilty for all the lies she had to tell her dad; and for having sex on the equipment at work; and for giving her baby away; and for those few days when she considered an abortion because how could she not? She was human.

Breakdown at a Consumer Value Store

She walked into a CVS after work one afternoon to buy some lotion and just started weeping. She just found herself standing in front of all the lotions on the lotion shelf in the lotion aisle of the CVS thought, "it is going to be just fucking impossible for me to pick out a fucking lotion." That was it. She just couldn't do it. It was just beyond the very bounds of what was possible. There was no way she was going to be able to pick out a lotion. There was no way she would ever have the intellectual and emotional wherewithal to choose between vanilla and lavender and unscented and regular scent. She just couldn't do it. The choices were insurmountable. So she just started weeping. Like an audible weeping that resulted in real tears rolling down her face. There was also the fluorescent lights and the garish way they shone light on her disheveled body and greasy hair and guilty and now red-splotched face; and the smell of the CVS that made her think of visiting CVS at home with her mom whenever she was sick and needed a prescription because apparently all CVS stores smell the same and her mom hadn't bought her all those prescriptions with money she earned from working for and taking orders from the highly demanding college professors so that she could get a paycheck and spend all that time raising her so that she could turn into a filthy fucking girl who got knocked up; that added to the whole scene.

One of the stock boys asked her if everything was ok and she said something akin to, "I just don't know anymore" and "I'm sorry I'm sorry" and she put her head on his shoulder and just wept and wept and wept and wept. She had feelings before – always had – but had never experienced feelings as iridescent pulsating living things that made her lose control. She just wanted to leave the entirety of her own self and jump into someone else's skin. Like the stock boy at CVS. She wanted to be the stock boy at CVS and just stock shelves all day and not even think about the lotions and creams and salves and how she had to rub them on her belly and then go home (any kind of home – she would have lived in a tree fort if it meant not being her and feeling the way she did right then) to watch TV (in her tree fort) and not think about anything or anyone.

The stock boy hugged her and patted her on the back and said "shhhhhh" over and over again and told her that it was going to be "OK" as though this thing happened every day. As though embracing and comforting patrons was part of a CVS stock boy's job description. Then the stock boy led her outside to her 1979 Oldsmobile Omega and asked her if she was ok to drive. She assured him she was and then she drove home and got upstairs and laid down on her couch and then realized that she hadn't even said "thank you" to the stock boy; hadn't even looked at his stock boy name tag and then had to cry and cry and cry all over again.

Ruth called to see how she was doing and she just started crying some more. Ruth said she would be over.

"Can you pick me up some lotion on your way over here?"

"Sure baby. What kind?"

"I don't care. Any kind. Any scent. Pumper or squeeze bottle. I don't even care. Water based or oil based I don't even think I have a preference. I don't ever think I ever have had a preference or ever will have a preference. I just can't do it today."

Ruth arrived about a half hour later; with some Vaseline Intensive Care lotion; and Pringles. Fucking CVS. Lotion and Pringles under one roof. Ruth sat with her as they ate Pringles and watched TV.

"Who eats Pringles?" Ruth asked.

"We do now. I guess." Gloria replied as she laid her head on Ruth's shoulder. Ruth patted her on her back. "Are you wiping your Pringles grease on my robe?"

"You know it babe."

114

Speeding

You know how when you meet someone famous and then you say, "He/She is just like us?" John Fitzgerald Kennedy, Jr. was not like that. He was enormously and profoundly unlike any collective us.

Of course, there were traits that his son might share with him. He hated mayonnaise. And could not help but love Christopher Cross and Roberta Flack and Prince. He loved Sheila E.'s "The Glamorous Life." And he loathed Steely Dan; the Doobie Brothers, and the Police. He loved McDonalds fries and pizza and Mexican food. But then you know how when you eat Mexican food and something from the burrito squirts onto your chin and you look gross? When sauces and salsas squirted out of John's burrito, he didn't look gross. He loved to read; loved adventure tales and myths; he couldn't tie a tie properly and always forgot his wallet and you know how sometimes you can mess up tying your tie and look slovenly.... well he never looked slovenly.

He loved dogs.

He had been to India and Africa; he had worked in a post-earthquake disaster zone in Guatemala for weeks and slept in tents and ate what the locals ate; when he drove too fast you still felt safe; when he shook your hand he looked at you differently; he was kind but not obsequious; he liked eggnog and pumpkin pie and cheap beer. It wasn't just confidence that came from travel and being part of *that* society; it was confidence that comes from being able to both dwell and excel in rarified circles, in the epicenters of wealth and power, while also being able to dwell and excel among anyone, earthquake victims in Guatemala for example, people living under apartheid. It was unclear to anyone who met him if what they were seeing was confidence or such profound humility because once you got to be him, confidence was of no consequence.

Fall

Her colleagues seemed oblivious to her state. No one asked her if she ok or told her that she hadn't been herself lately. Either she was a good actress or her colleagues lacked empathy or archive librarians were inherently moody and her colleagues *did* detect the changes to her mood but attributed it to the inherent moodiness of archivist librarians. Or maybe people were genuinely reticent to ask women if everything was ok because they did not want to offend or wade into areas of biology. Who knows. Oddly though, she found their ambivalence comforting. Even as she sat at her desk and the simplest tasks were suddenly impossibly gargantuan, she enjoyed the rhythms and the routines and the challenges of her job. She liked that it was necessary for her to get out of bed in the morning.

She had appointment with a doctor friend of Ruth's at the hospital.

"Everything looks fine," he said.

Gary M. Almeter

Yesterday Once More

She went home for Thanksgiving. Her first time back in Homer since Christmas 1982. It was odd; but the reason it was odd is because of how normal it all was. Like life proceeded for everyone else at exactly the same rate and cadence and trajectory that it should. The light still hit the same pieces of furniture and same floors and rugs in her parents' home at all the same angles and at all the same times. Homer was exactly the same, not quite a small town and not quite a suburb and not quite sure of what it wanted to be. It was disorienting for her to arrive home and see that life elsewhere had not changed. And while things for her had been less than predictable and less than normal, she astonished herself at how easily she could pretend that nothing happened; how she could accept their earnestness and their curiosity with nary a hiccup.

"Is everything good with you sweetie?" her dad asked.

"Yeah dad. Everything's good. You good?"

"You sure, Sweetie?"

"Why? Does it seem like I'm not doing well?"

"No no no. Not at all. I guess I just miss you."

Her dad. He felt sorry for her. He imagined that her life in Providence was hard – doing research for Ivy League folks and walking up two flights of stairs to an empty apartment after work and what did she even do when she got home and making meals for one person and what is that even like? He felt sorry for her because she could no longer live the same life in Homer that he loved and was so proud of. Meanwhile, Gloria felt sorry for all of them because they were stuck in a perpetual living breathing time capsule doing the things they had always done and always did and always will do. But she knew that would have also loved being back home in the status quo she pretended to loathe. There was something very comforting about knowing that some things will never ever change. But she knew that there was also something very jarring about wanting to be elsewhere – any elsewhere anywhere at all – and then arriving at that elsewhere and discovering that the elsewhere you envisioned was not so spectacular and you go back to the point from which you yearned to escape and find comfort.

She loved Providence; she loved Ruth; she loved her job. But the circumstances of the last few months made her wonder if she even knew what she had been hoping for. Adventure? Independence? A change of scenery? Check all those boxes. So now what was she supposed to do? Maybe being an adult is just inherently difficult she thought. Or this in-between space of not being a child but not quite being fully independent. She was still driving her dad's car.

Thanksgiving Day was tough, accepting hugs and kisses and accolades from grandparents who would surely be appalled and disgusted if they knew what she had done.

Leaving home is not an event. It's not packing a pair of cars and answering your dad's questions about where you want the coat rack; it's a lengthy, protracted process; a condition. You leave home triumphantly and the rest of your life will be plagued by an invisible force luring you back, to sleep in a twin bed underneath the posters and trophies you had as a kid. She thought this as she looked out her childhood bedroom window now and saw the same big maple tree she looked at when she was a kid; on the same bed she had had since she moved out of her crib when her cousin Paul was born and her aunt and uncle needed a crib; as she lied underneath the Afghan her grandma crocheted for her a zig zag pattern consisting of four shades of red, four shades of blue and four shades of white. Her grandma crocheted it for the 1976 bicentennial.

There were still dolls piled onto an old desk in the corner of her room; remnants from when she was a little girl. There was an empty pack of cigarettes in her top desk drawer – a souvenir from when her friend Nancy and she had stolen a pack of cigarettes from the dashboard of a car parked in church and smoked the remaining cigarettes in back of Nancy's house. Nancy called her house Wednesday night and asked her mom if Gloria was coming home for Thanksgiving and if she was to give her a call back. Gloria hadn't called her back and wouldn't. There were posters on the wall of the Bee Gees, Jimmy Osmond, John McEnroe (and as she looked at the poster she realized that his red, white and blue headband matched nicely with her Grandma's red, white and blue zig zag Afghan), a Donna Summer poster, and a poster of the cover of Pink Floyd's Dark Side of the Moon album. There are also ribbons from the Cortland County Fair – 8 blue, 11 red and 3 white projects she did with her local 4-H group – the Homer Hummingbirds. They made throw pillows and terrariums and needlepoint. Her room had outdated floral wallpaper and a pink shag carpet of which she had been so proud when her parents let her pick it out as a birthday present. And trophies for being a mathlete and for participation in *It's Academic* in Syracuse in 1977 and 1978.

She thought about all the things she had been. The woman she was in November 1983. All the things she was not. She was not many things and she felt so old already, as though time was running out. She had never hitch hiked. Had never been to India; or New Zealand; or Paris; or South America; or London; or Russia; or Africa; or anywhere outside of the United States except for a class trip to Niagara Falls once where they briefly crossed over into Canada. She had never seen Pink Floyd in concert nor seen John McEnroe play tennis. She had seen Jimmy Osmond in concert along with his brothers and one sister, Marie. They played at the New York State fair one year and she had also seen Karen Carpenter in Saratoga in 1976. She had never seen the Bee Gees or Journey or the Police. She had only slept with four men. She had never been water skiing; or sky diving; or hang gliding. She had never been to a professional sporting event of any kind. Though she had seen the Syracuse Orangemen play plenty of times in the heralded Carrier Dome. She had never drag raced or done LSD or cocaine.

She still had so much to do.

While out shopping with her mother for a new winter coat, they ran into Mrs. Perry, the mother of a friend of hers who had a son who died about six years prior. He was about 10 years older than Gloria and her friend and died from alcohol poisoning. She had heard Mrs. Perry on the phone shortly after he died say, "Alcohol addiction is stronger than a mother's love." She looked as sad on this November 1983 afternoon as she had the day of her son's funeral. The family was never really the same again.

Gary M. Almeter

Nothing Changes on New Year's Day

Astonishingly, Gloria was sad to say goodbye to 1983. This surprised even her. She was determined to embrace every New Year trope and make a new start, but when she told herself to move on she still did not know how to reconcile all of the what happened before with what happens now. The past was suddenly this big, huge dark deep place in which she would always feel partially submerged. At least that's how she felt New Year's Eve. She was completely unaware – emotionally, cognitively, mentally – how to move on. Forget the past. Impossible.

Maybe it was time to accept that if people are the sum of all their experiences then last year's experiences would be far more crucial in determining who she was to be.

Ruth asked her if she wanted to go to a party– some of her hospital friends were getting together at another nurse's house and there would be doctors there and the whole thing. Gloria declined, content to watch Dick Clark's New Year's Rockin' Eve; she wanted to have all her faculties and to be fully cogent when 1983 slipped into the past. She needed to see it; she needed to take a deep breath and see how it felt; she needed a guarantee that it happened. She needed to see it. That 1983 was now in the past tense.

Plus Laura Branigan was performing, inevitably singing her song "Gloria."

When it happened – when the ball in Times Square dropped – she toasted the air and had a sip of wine and smiled. The next day she would write down a couple of resolutions,

"Reconcile the past." "No more self-pity." "Try not to think of John (aside from the standard level of interest afforded him by the general public.)"

Outsiders

Providence did not get as much snow as Gloria was accustomed to and, she was discovering, enjoyed. In Homer she hated when it snowed, especially when she was commuting to Syracuse. But when she wasn't so reliant on a car, she rather liked it. Liked the tranquility and the beauty of it.

Ruth was officially dating someone she met at work. A doctor named Will. Gloria was genuinely happy for her and really liked him when she met him, when the three of them went to dinner on Valentine's Day. When she told Ruth in the rest room to marry him Ruth laughed in that way that said she was already determined to do so. Gloria imagined what Ruth's marriage might mean to their friendship. Their time together would inevitably be diminished. Nothing would *happen*; there would be no falling out or skirmish or identifiable moment when a fissure became a schism or anything. They would just start leading different lives; Ruth would invite Gloria to parties and spend time introducing her to their married friends and neighbors; then a child's first birthday and Ruth and the moms she had met at lactation class would laugh at the way the kids ate cake and Gloria would wonder what they were laughing at because is a kid eating cake really that funny?

That of course, presumed that she would not be married her own self. And she sort of figured she wouldn't be. Certainly not anytime soon. If ever. She knew that one day she would consider herself worthy of that sort of life; she also imagined when she would have *that conversation* with whomever she got close to marrying. At what point would that be? Their first date; make it a threshold criterion like height or education or whatever other factors people used as benchmarks of dateability? "I've had a baby and gave him up for adoption." OK. Simple enough. But there would surely be some inevitable follow-up questions. Would she lie when he asked her who the father was? She certainly couldn't trust a man with whom she was on a first date to keep a secret like that. When they got serious? When does that happen? She had a "serious" boyfriend in high school but their problems generally consisted of deciding in which parking lot in which to hang out on Friday night. Anyway, there is always the risk that any beau she might have would find the information – that she had a baby and gave him up for adoption – came too early or too late. There would be this moment in the relationship which would mark the perfect time to tell him. If she told him too early then he might run away and if she told him too late then he might be offended that she waited that long. She would be in a perpetual state of something akin to Goldilocks – wondering if the bed was too small or too big and if the porridge was too hot or too cold – wondering if she was telling him too soon or too late.

Or what if she didn't tell him at all? Then, she wondered, if twenty or thirty years later when people were talking on watches and driving flying cars and generally living like Jetsons, then her son would locate her, knock on her door, her husband would answer, and he'd be will be all "Does Gloria Winegar live here?" and the imaginary husband would be all, "Why yes it is and who the fuck are you?" and he would say "I am Gloria's son." And then after everyone got everything "all sorted out" the husband might get mad or at best, be merely hurt that his wife hadn't trusted him enough to tell him this large bit of information.

But that inaugural question, "Well, who's the father?" would prompt a whole additional set of conundrums. Would she lie and manufacture a name like Joe Schmo from high school or Billy McDilly from down the street? Or would she lie and say she didn't know – that it could be any number of people as he was conceived during what Gloria would gleefully refer to as her "promiscuous period"? Then what? Who would want to continue a relationship with someone who went through a "promiscuous period"? And went through it gleefully no less?

Or she could tell him the truth, the whole truth, and nothing but the truth. But then what if it's so early in the relationship that he does a quick cost benefit analysis and determines it would be worth it to discard her and sell the story, a juicy story, to the National Enquirer? And then what? Then life as she knew it would be over. Life as lots of people knew it would be over. "Maybe people will be less infatuated with celebrity in the future than they are now in 1984" she told herself.

She finally landed on that she would just know when she met the right man what she should do. Though she would also test him first – tell him the father of her baby was Tom Selleck or Loverboy lead singer Mike Reno, and gauge his reaction from that. She would have to first do some research – which would not be difficult as she was a librarian after all – and discover when Loverboy toured in 1982. She knew they gave a concert in Syracuse a few years ago. Yes. She snuck backstage after a Loverboy concert and got impregnated by Mike Reno, lead singer of Loverboy. Think of the jokes they could make about the lead singer of a band named Loverboy?

But why sell herself short? Matt Dillon. Emilio Estevez. Tom Cruise. Rob Lowe. Really any cast member of *The Outsiders*.

She decided she would cross that bridge when she came to it.

Life is filled with "tough conversations;" she understood that. She also realized that she had no idea what she might want in a husband. Her dad had been a great example of what a husband should be. Though she recalled her mother as being perpetually weary: perpetually putting towels underneath the door to stop drafts, perpetually cutting coupons, perpetually wiping up puddles left from snowy boots while talking about the futility of wiping up puddles, perpetually reminding them all to finish their food that there were hungry kids in China. Gloria wondered if children from Beijing would ever want to switch places with her. All the snow in Homer, the puddles left on the floor from snowy boots, the drafts that blew into the house from underneath the old door. Did they even have such oppressive cold in Beijing?

Keep Your Feet on the Ground

Ruth was supportive. She did what she could, said what she could. There were days though when Gloria felt like the support she required was more akin to being strapped to a dolly and being wheeled around rather than mere encouragement. No one ever physically propped her up which is what she felt like she needed at times. There were times she lived in segments, looking forward to tasks and events where she knew she'd be occupied for a few hours. Like the movies. Or listening to Kasey Casem's Top 40 on Sunday afternoons.

Watering the Lawn

Every now and again, Ruth would ask her, "what was he like?"

"Well he saluted his dad's coffin on his third birthday. He had a lot of hair. He grew up in New York City."

"I already know all that. Tell me things I don't know."

"Why?"

"Just because. He must be more interesting than that."

"How does it get more interesting than that?"

"You know what I mean. I mean interesting as authentic."

"He was really really funny. He liked Elvis Costello. He had this weird disdain for people who watered their lawns. He mentioned it to me twice. He was like, 'It's just a lawn. Get over it.' I thought that was interesting."

A Few Bobby Pins

People tended to be surprised when she told them that she was an archivist at Brown. Even in a town where everyone seemed to have some connection to the university – an aunt or uncle or cousin who worked there or maybe even went there. While she did not look like she stepped out of a Slim Aarons photo – no caftan, no plunging neckline pantsuit – she apparently was better looking than what people typically associated with librarians.

"But recall the scene in *It's a Wonderful Life*" she would say, "when George Bailey is in the midst of seeing what life is like without him and he sees Mary Baily – an unmarried librarian – and she went from hot to not hot with just a few bobby pins and a pair of glasses, and a drab suit."

She would stay at her job as an archivist at Brown University's library, for the entirety of her career. She did so because she liked it, sure; because the benefits of working at an Ivy League university were crazy good – health insurance, dental, vision, prescription, tuition remission, time off; her commute was easy; she liked Providence. She also would have been lying to herself had she said that those embers of hope she maintained that he – either of the *hes*, the son she left with the nuns or the man who fathered him – would be able to find her if she stayed where she was did not factor into her decision to stay, or decision not to leave, or general non-decision to even entertain thoughts about leaving; that staying put somehow meant that should he – either of the he's to whom she had recently said goodbye – would one day come down the stairs into the John Hay Library's subterranean archives department and say "hello." She entertained myriad thoughts like this; scores of such thoughts. Which also meant that there was a modicum of a tinge of something resembling disappointment every day one of them did not descend the stairs.

She refused to adhere or succumb or otherwise comply with or observe the stereotypes associated with the single librarian. She never got a cat and she never learned how to knit and she refused to wear slacks that had elastic. She wore cool loafers and clothes she considered stylish. Thanks to *Dallas* big hair and shoulder pads were all the rage; she adopted a more youthful look, jeans and sweaters and a general Ivy League gestalt.

And besides, as mentioned above, she liked the job. Or liked it enough. They call it work for a reason, right? Her father probably hadn't enjoyed fixing and greasing and maintain and tightening and calibrating things on the Smith Corona assembly line right? Making typewriters upon which others would muse and write and speculate and pontificate. And how "fun" had her mom had typing letters and taking dictation and transcribing department meetings and arranging flights to academic conventions? She majored in this because she liked it right? Because of her whole Chester Gillette *A Place in the Sun* connection, right? Sure it also helped that her mom worked in the department at Syracuse and had shepherded her application through and gave her access to the "best" professors.

She had tried adventure. She had seduced a student. And look what her need for independence and adventure had brought her. No. She was fine staying put. Even if it felt like penance at times.

Rocky Road

There were weeks when she still got sad; weeks when hygiene was challenging; when she went to bed as soon as she got home from work; when she ate potato chips and Snickers bars and doughnuts and Rocky Road ice cream and Twizzlers and the one-pound bags of peanut M & Ms and wash them all down with wine. There were weeks she listened to nothing but Air Supply and Barry Manilow and weeks when she listened to nothing at all and weeks when she just incessantly hit the radio's scan button. There were weeks when she neglected to water her Ficus and did nothing as its leaves withered and fell off, as if powerless to prevent the withering. There were weeks when she wore socks thrice before taking them off and weeks when she drank nothing but Dr. Pepper and wine and ordered pizza three or four nights a week and ate leftover pizza the nights she didn't order fresh pizza; weeks she did not vacuum and did not iron and did not clean her bath room and did not moisturize or tweeze or brush.

During those times, she tried to identify but could never discern what portion of her malaise, if any, was attributable to *what happened* and what portion of her malaise was due to just being human, due to the rigors and defeats and frustrations and setbacks and disappointments of just being alive, and what portion of her malaise might be attributable to her own deleterious behaviors. And of that portion of malaise she might have attributed to her own behavior, how to *further subdivide and allocate* that portion between those things she was doing wrong (was she not going out enough? Should she get a different hairstyle? Did she live too far from mom and dad? Was she at fault for not yet calling and considering Providence *home?* Did she eat wrong? Drink too much or too little? Was she in the wrong profession?) and those things unique to her but not of her doing, i.e., the way the chemicals and the wires and synapses in her brain did or did not function or engage one another, or fired too robustly or not robustly enough and the way she was raised and the genes she inherited that made her predisposed to being moody and likely depressed.

Every now and again, she and Ruth would go for a drive. Just to get out of the city. Just 20-30 minutes outside of Providence, a few miles away from Brown University, were people about whom she had forgotten: people whose pets were Rottweilers and whose Rottweilers were perpetually chained to rusty, long-dormant Chevy pickups; people dwelling – not so much dwelling as enduring – in shacks. The span between living and enduring was 20 minutes then apparently. But was she doing more than enduring? More than existing?

She remembered being a little girl in Homer and thinking McDonald's was a treat.

Gary M. Almeter

"...as if he were unrecognizable."

John had never told anyone about Gloria either. He never talked about his girlfriends, or *partners.* Had the paparazzi not stalked him and followed him and taken his picture with Darryl Hannah and Sarah Jessica Parker and Cindy Crawford, *et al.,* no one would have known he was ever with these women either. So he didn't not talk about Gloria because she was Gloria, he just didn't talk about **anyone** with whom he had been intimate. He thought of her from time to time. Though after a few years it took him a moment or two to recall her name. If the memory of her lingered for more than the few seconds of recall, he would try to remember what she sounded like, looked like, smelled like. All of this diminished as the years went by. It's just what happens. And life for him proceeded at a much faster pace than most; he would have liked for it to slow down. He would have liked to be ordinary.

He went to India after college for a while after college and reveled in the rare prolonged anonymity. In New York City, where he was going to law school, he tasted anonymity from time to time, those minutes roller blading in Central Park before someone recognized him as even a helmet could not conceal his dark curly hair; a strategically placed hat and sunglasses bought him a few cherished minutes if he left his apartment at the right time. If he biked far and fast enough he could feel that no one was watching him. If he canoed or kayaked or rowed far enough he could feel genuine solitude. Though it was always fleeting.

It was not surprising to those who knew him that he would want to try flying.

Walking to Work

Her apartment was becoming home. But it did suffer the rare double defect of being both too close and too far from the John Hay library. It was close enough that she could walk easily and comfortably on pleasant days but also far enough away that if she walked on rainy days she would arrive soaked or if she walked on those days following a snowfall, she would arrive with frozen feet, as her warm boots were not suited for walking. However, it was also too close to buy a monthly parking pass to which employees of the university were then-entitled; and driving even on the rainy days felt a tad indulgent. Almost silly. So she walked almost every day. And over the years in which she lived on Benevolent Street and worked at the John Hay library, learned which sidewalks were adjacent to large water puddles in the street and the routes with which she could avoid them; which boots could simultaneously repel water and cold while also still provide for comfort and flexibility; which sides of which streets got the sunlight when it was just chilly enough to make her want to walk in sunshine and which sides of which streets were shaded when it was just warm enough to make her want to walk in the shade; which iterations of snack bars and Tupperware and pretzels fit in which lunch boxes and how she would have to alternate shoulders while carrying a 14 ounce can of soup along with a hardcover copy of Stephen King's *Christine* or carrying a bottle of salad dressing to replenish the one in the employee refrigerator along with a copy of James Michener's *Space* so her shoulders don't ache by the time she got to work.

There was a day, however, that she realized — or feared - that it happened to everyone. Commuters on every commuter train knew just where to stand so that the doors of the Metro North or New Jersey Transit or Chicago El opened right before them; drivers who knew precisely which lanes to drive in to avoid cars turning left, which shortcuts to take during which weather, and which radio stations played commercial free music at which stages in the commute to maximize music and minimize advertisements.

And she realized that she wasn't special. That no one was really special. That everyone was just doing the best they could.

Say That You Remember

Every September Gloria took a day off, maybe had some ice cream, and take some minutes to purposefully reflect on what the baby she had might be doing. She would ask herself a zillion questions. Kids start kindergarten at age five right? Did he take a bus to school like she did or did he live close enough to walk? If he had a lunch box, what was on the lunch box, what he was into? Star Wars? Snoopy? Did kids still get into Snoopy?

Dinosaurs? Hockey? Boston Bruins? Gremlins? Kids probably didn't get into Gremlins at age 5. But she didn't have a good gauge on what kids did. Batman? Zoo animals? Farm animals? Aquatic mammals? Fish?

She and Ruth were out to dinner on one of these September birthdays.

"What do you want, Gloria? Like have you determined that? Have you sat down and said, 'This is what I want.'?"

"Yes. I Just want to be normal again. I want to stop thinking about this and have a family – what the fuck do families even do now. Frolic in piles of their disposable income? Argue about pool memberships? Argue about creamy versus crunchy peanut butters? Go to Disney World every year? I want to argue about peanut butter."

"We are seeing a ton more kids with peanut allergies now so you might never get to argue about peanut butter."

"Jesus. Of all the best friends in the world and I get the obstetrics nurse who thinks she's an allergist."

"Yeah lucky you."

"Lucky me." They toasted to this notion with their wine glasses. "I don't have a list of what I want. I'm fine with no Volvo and no backyard and no in-ground pool."

"Well you wouldn't have to argue about pool memberships if you had your own in-ground pool"

"And I'm fine with no Disney World. But I want someone to belong to me. I want to have sex. I just want what every other idiot in America wants." Gloria demanded.

"No one knows what they want, Gloria."

"Everyone knows what they want. It's just that what they want isn't necessarily what's right for them. But even if you're right – even if no one knows what they want – they know it when they see it. Like you weren't necessarily looking for Will. You didn't know you wanted Will. But then you met him. And you wanted him. Right?"

"That's accurate."

"So to answer your initial question, I want to be in a position to know what I want when I see it. And it's not easy."

Pitch Forks

Her grandpa told her a story once about this time he and two of his brothers were playing in the hay loft when they were kids, "I was probably 9 or 10." He said. "We were climbing on the hay bales, running and jumping around and so forth. Kid stuff. My brother Ralph, he was probably 7 or 8, lost his balance when he jumped onto a pile of bales and he fell and was impaled on the pitch forks that we had stuck into a bale down on the ground."

Ralph died after spending the night in agony.

Gloria's grandpa told her that story with the nonchalance of someone who might have been describing a visit to a pizzeria; or a fishing trip. He wasn't cold about it. It was just a fact of life that people died.

She remembered this whenever she asked herself why she couldn't move on and it made things worse. Some people can watch other people, people they love, get impaled on pitch forks and move on with ease; some people can go to war and come home and proceed as if their wartime experience had been a slight detour; some people can have children and give them away and move on.

She couldn't.

Sowing the Seeds of Love

Gloria was in the grocery store when she saw a *People* magazine with JFK Jr. on the cover. The magazine identified him as the "The Sexiest Man Alive."

She knew there would be a day like this – she did not know that he would ever be identified as the Sexiest Man Alive but she had known or suspected there would be a day where he would be lauded, or heralded, or otherwise celebrated, for something. That the natural progression of his public life, his *persona,* that started at commencement would inevitably lead to a public life more, well, *public.* She had also learned – was certain of it despite what she thought of as her ineptitude in most things associated with life - that it was possible to feel multiple emotions simultaneously and that the feeling of one did not diminish the other.

She experienced many emotions when she saw him on the cover of *People* magazine's heralded "Sexiest Man Alive" issue. She was giddy. Is that an emotion? She thought so. "I feel giddy." She was happy. She felt sad for him, knowing that he would find such a proclamation classless, unrefined, and the attention unwarranted and that such attention should be directed elsewhere. She was not ashamed that she was proud that they were once intimate. She was a little turned on. She remembered, fondly, what those weeks of intimacy with him were like. Presumably he had not suffered the same dearth of intimacy from which she had suffered since 1983. Suffered is the wrong here. She was content being solo. Wasn't she? She wasn't suffering. She was enjoying time alone. She was also a little angry that she couldn't tell people about their intimacy.

Her parents were placing new emphasis on her own marital status. She was in her late twenties. Her sister was married and her brother was engaged. She would have loved to tell them that she and JFK Jr. had "done it; frequently" to make them jealous; to make them stop feeling sorry for her; to make them stop talking about their bridal registries and rehearsal dinners at Homer's local VFW and volunteer fire department community halls.

Sometimes her intellectual curiosity went a different way. What if she had told John that she was pregnant? What if she had told him that she was pregnant and that they had to get married or he had to give her 10 million dollars? Or 5 million? Or maybe just 2 million? Or, fuck it, 20 million? What would have happened? If she had asked for 20 million dollars to stay quiet, what would have happened? She typically landed on, he likely would have given her $10 million and made her sign some sort of confidentiality agreement and then she would have been on her way. But maybe not. He was famous but not heartless. Theirs wasn't a tryst forbidden by some Mafioso. So maybe what if Gloria had told him she was pregnant and when he heard he recalled the feelings which led him into her arms in the first place and they got married? She would be a Kennedy. Alternatively, and here is where her mind gets really nefarious, what if he had rejected her and stunned by this, she went to the media and sold her story for millions? She would be wealthy. And famous. Or infamous. She'd be lumped together with Donna Rice and Fawn Hall and Jessica Hahn. People would talk about Donna Rice and Fawn Hall and Jessica Hahn and Gloria Winegar as the women of the 80s who brought down powerful men. She would not have been a good Donna Rice. Or what if John had had her killed? He hadn't given off those vibes though, those "I'm going to kill my lover when it gets inconvenenient" vibes.

When her sister got married, to a Phys Ed teacher at Homer High School, she tried to be happy for her. She was careful not to drink too much at the reception for fear of getting so wasted that she, whenever some great aunt asked her, "when are you going to get hitched?" she didn't say something like, "Bitch if you knew the dick I've had and what I've done you'd relax a little bit on the whole marriage thing. And guess what else? I don't want to marry a Homer High School Phys Ed teacher and launder sweatpants and make basketball games and fucking bake sales my whole fucking life." Not that she had thought about it. Not that she was bitter.

Did she sound bitter? It was likely a nice potpourri of bitterness, exhaustion, sadness, and frustration. She was learning that jealousy turned to resentment and resentment turned to anger with relative ease. Sometimes she looked around and felt so envious that she thought she might explode. Every single person she saw seemed like they are on the cusp of something extraordinary; nearly all the students for whom she worked could literally do almost anything they wanted to do – move to Manhattan after graduation? Sure thing! Move to Europe after graduation? Why not? Move to Los Angeles and try your hand at screenwriting? Practically encouraged!! Take some time off and travel the world and maybe stop in India to feed the poor and photograph the poor Indians and submit those photographs to your classmate's father who runs Doubleday books and get them published? Definitely!! Explore, delve, scrutinize, traverse, travel, tour, burrow, dare, probe, wander, negotiate, deviate, postulate, ruminate. Why not?

Later that year Ruth got married. She married a doctor, William. They waited until William knew exactly where he would be practicing and were elated when he discovered that he had been matched at the hospital where had done his residency, the same one where Ruth worked. Gloria was maid of honor and thought the doctor perfect for Ruth. She was also pleasantly amazed at how little things had changed between she and Ruth during the whole courtship and engagement thing. Doctors worked long days and nights and when Ruth's husband was working those long nights, Ruth and Gloria had fun.

Nonetheless, Gloria started dating.

It was not fun.

Ruth practiced dating with her one evening.

"Practice question," Ruth began. "What makes you happy?"

"Well the last time I was happy was when I wore a Benetton rugby to work and someone thought I was a student."

"Ok." Ruth said dejectedly. "Let's start with something simpler. What do you do for fun?"

"I drink eggnog."

"That is not what people do for fun, Gloria. What about normal things?"

"Like what normal things?"

"I don't know like puppies and Princess Diana and shopping."

"I don't do Princess Diana for fun."

"Damn you Gloria."

She dated a guy who liked to get high and listen to Tears for Fears before they went out. Gloria, as she learned, was happy to try anything once. So she tried getting high and listening to Tears for Fears. She understood the multi-layered synthesizers and sounds of Tears for Fears could be considered interesting while high. But it just wasn't her thing.

She was not surprised at how picky she was but she was surprised at the things she identified as deal breakers. She went on a date with a guy who wore a too-tight turtleneck that showed his nipples; a date with a guy who used the end of his fork to scratch an itch on his cheek while eating his Caesar salad; a guy who did all the Oak Ridge Boys voices while he sang along to "Elvira;" a guy with a "They Will Get My Gun When They Pry My Cold Dead Finger Off The Trigger" bumper sticker on his car; a guy who wore a Rubik's Cube sweatshirt on their date; a guy who finished her entrée; a guy who had four beers at dinner; she went on a date with a guy who shushed her when Eddie Murphy's "Party All the Time" came on the radio. She looked at him and said, "This isn't going to work. Turn the car around and take me home." Getting shushed was one thing; getting shushed so the man could listen to a six-minute song with the same verse over and over again was quite another. And spend $1.99 on the fucking *cassingle* if you like the song so much asshole. She went on a date with a guy who had seen *Top Gun* "more than three dozen times" and told her, "if things go well we can go home and watch it on my big screen tv; the stereo makes it sound like the jets are flying right over your head." She wanted to ask him if things went really really well they could play volleyball on the beach wearing dungarees. But figured such passive aggressive teasing would have gone right over his head; like a Navy fighter jet driven by Iceman. Or piloted? Jets are piloted not driven she thought to herself as she tried to mentally escape that man.

She was encouraged by this – she was getting better at dating it seemed. Despite the duds. The fact that she still had standards; that she could voice those standards; that she was still 'herself' and that she could still hope for more. Or someone she liked.

"Guys are fucking crazy," she told Ruth.

"We're pretty crazy too."

"Everyone is fucking crazy then."

Roller Blading in Central Park

John dated who he liked; which isn't to say he dated *whomever* he liked. Some women said no to him, citing the complete and total upheaval of their own status quo in their always polite declinations. John dated only women he liked, or suspected he might like, or suspected he wanted to know better.

He listened to the music he liked (Eurythmics, Smiths, Cure, Prince, Pet Shop Boys, and yes, Springsteen and Bon Jovi now and again; Elvis still had not grown on him) he ate the foods he liked and he read the books he liked. He went to the schools he liked and talked to the people he liked. He dated the women he liked. He dated Daryl Hannah because he liked her. How else to explain it? There was no cost benefit analysis, no conjecture, no marketing surveys; at least not from him. He met her, got a good gut feeling, and asked her out. It was not a statement about blondes or actresses or tall women. Him wearing a brown coat did not mean he was anti-blue coat; him roller blading in Central Park did not mean that he considered joggers or kayakers or bicyclists less than; him ordering a hamburger did not mean he was anti-hot dog.

People just like what they like. John knew this.

"The Hunk Flunks"

When he failed his bar exam the second time, three New York newspapers trumpeted the news of her son's father's failure on their front pages. Each of the headlines was some derivation of the phrase, "The Hunk Flunks." The Daily News made it clear that this is his second time failing the bar exam and in the photograph, John's surprise at seeing the photographers made him look childish and fearful and guilty.

It was not easy to, when asked about the indignity by a phalanx of reporters, reply innocuously, "I am very disappointed, again. God willing, I will be back (to take the test) in July. I am clearly not a legal genius." Then he said to the reporters, "Next time you guys are here, I hope it will be a happy day." What a classy thing to say to those parasites. If they only knew how hard the New York State bar exam was. Lots of people fail it; lots of people fail it twice; lots of people fail it thrice. Some people never pass it.

Participating

Gloria neither participated nor had any interest in the dramas (library employee break room skirmishes regarding unwashed spoons left in the sink and replenishing coffee filters; her mother's tirades about how thank you notes from her sister's soon-to-be-in-laws were too terse; her fellow tenants' letters to their landlord regarding sidewalk snow removal) or the drama (the Tiananmen Squares, the Roseanne Barr massacring the

National Anthem, the Exxon Valdez, the Dan Quayle misspelling potato and criticizing Murphy Brown for her reproductive choices, the Ayatollah Khomeini's skirmish with Salman Rushdie) of the day. She fancied herself immune to it all; fancied herself victorious if she got through the day without breaking down.

Until there was a day this changed.

Then there was a day when she realized that any specialness, any aura, any excuse she had been using for not doing and moving and progressing had dissipated, like the days after Christmas when you realize it's not Christmas anymore. When you see a Christmas tree in a neighbor's house and think how odd they still have their Christmas tree up? There's no specific time allotted for this post-celebratory period but "you're supposed to know it when you know it" she thought.

This saddened her; she enjoyed having a reason to procrastinate; to be still; to lounge and engage in something resembling self-pity. She was not sure when that day, this transition between special and normal, happened.

But it did.

Peyton Place

Gloria was turning the basement of the John Hay library at Brown University into her own Peyton Place apparently. She met someone there, and while she did not fornicate with him on the microfiche machine, they did go out on a few dates. Yet. They did not fornicate on top of the microfiche machine yet.

His name was Arun, Professor Arun Reddy. He was a professor of American race and ethnicity, part of the Sociology department, an Indian man. He was tall and wore monogrammed shirts and khakis and tortoiseshell glasses. While not the type for which she might ordinarily go, she got the shivers or goose bumps or whatever they were at the back of her neck when they started talking. And wait a minute "not the type for which she might ordinarily go" suggested that she had "gone for" people in the past. That she had a history of sleeping with exclusively mustachioed men; or men who drive big trucks; or men who are Italian or Croatian or Zimbabwean. To say that Arun was not her type was akin to saying that dinosaurs do not like Italian food. They've never had Italian food so how would one even know this? There was nothing to indicate that dinosaurs might like Italian food so saying that they don't like was not patently untrue but it's also not supported by any facts.

She just hadn't regularly dated someone in a while. Regularly and enthusiastically.

And it happened serendipitously. He came to the basement of John Hay and asked to see some documents from right-wing Christian religious organizations in the Hall-Hoag collection of dissenting and extremist printed propaganda. He was researching the papers Lester Garfield Maddox, Sr., who she learned, was an Atlanta restaurant owner who refused to serve blacks.

They met in May and before he left, as he tapped the manila folder filled with newly printed documents on the archive desk counter, asked if she would be working all summer as he planned on spending a "sizable amount" (his words, not hers; words which she found to be very alluring) of time there this summer on his latest research project. About Lester Maddox and the evolution of right wing and racist propaganda.

She found herself thinking about him and each day, wondering if that day would be a day he stopped in.

Cumberland Island

John Kennedy and Carolyn Bessette got married on September 21, 1996. No one knew about it, so details were scant at first. Then a furor started, the way that Americans start furors over things for which furos might not quite be necessary. Furors over the people they proclaim to love because they love them. Ostensibly.

There was quite a preoccupation with the wedding, the planning for which had been in the works for months. John and Carolyn even staged a fight in Central Park to get paparazzi off their tail. Then they flew everyone down to Cumberland Island and got married in an old slave church with just candles. Wow. "That Carolyn is one lucky lady," Gloria thought. "And so is he."

"She's beautiful – if you are into that sort of thing. I guess," she acceded. To herself and herself alone.

Marriage

John liked being married. A lot. His understanding of what it meant to be a husband was a little rudimentary in light of the fact that didn't really remember any interactions between his mother and father prior to his father's assassination; had lived most of life with a single mother; and didn't really observe much that he could use from his stepfather, Greek shipping tycoon Aristotle Onassis. His uncles had been helpful; until his Uncle Bob was assassinated; and Uncle Ted was a blast and he genuinely loved him but his life with Joan has been a little tumultuous and things with Vicki were still brand new.

When they, early on in their dating narrative, shared with one another all the people they slept with, he mentioned a librarian at Brown. And Carolyn did that thing of when you fake gasp and pretend to be astounded but you're really not. The librarian did not warrant a follow up question. Why ask about an anonymous librarian when you can ask about Madonna? And she had her own past partners and she was deciding on how to gingerly address them. How do you tell the sexiest man alive that you lost your virginity to a boy with acne in high school?

But he liked her. He liked marriage. He liked everything about her. He liked belonging to someone.

Piper Saratoga

When she woke up on July 17, 1999, she ambled into her kitchen on Benevolent Street to make coffee. She got a call from Ruth.

"Did you hear?"

"Hear what?"

"Fuck."

"What's happening, Ruth?"

"Turn on CNN babe. Let me know if you need anything."

"OK."

"Bye sweetie."

She wondered what her son was doing that day, wondering what boys on the cusp of sixteen did on a mid-summer's Saturday morning. Riding bicycles to the quarry? Or to the lake? Or to the pier? Or the jetty? Or maybe you are in someone's basement trading baseball cards? Or waking up from a long night drinking beer in a classmate's basement? Was he hung over? Do 15-year-olds still drink? Or was he more of a Dungeons and Dragons type of kid? Did he smoke? Did he have a girlfriend? Play lacrosse? Football? Beach volleyball? What are you doing this summer? Lifeguarding? Mowing lawns? Landscaping?

[As it happened Jay Kirby, as her son was then known, was on his way to work as a water slide attendant at Water Wizz, an amusement park just over the bridge from his house in Sandwich,

MA, on Cape Cod. While the fleets of news vans with the satellite dishes on top were going the other way, towards Hyannis Port, the general chaos of the scene on and at and near the bridge caused some congestion and he was late for work that day. So her son was not oblivious to what the rest of America was digesting and cognizing this morning. His mom had told him, while pouring him some orange juice and watching her small television in the kitchen – the one that still used rabbit ears –that a man named JFK Jr. was missing.]

He would now never know him, she tought to herself. Her son would never know his dad and the dad would never even become aware of the existence of the son. She had always imagined - less of an imagining and more of some sort of hazy mirage idea of a certainty – that while they would surely never enjoy a Thanksgiving dinner or Christmas eve together, that they would somehow be in the presence of one another and aware of each other. Did that make her crazy? Or merely human?

There was lots of talk on the news about his legacy and his magazine and how he had no children. All this talk amidst photos of the nearly perfectly spherical torrents that helicopters create when they hover over the water and scores of caring though not altogether not voyeuristic people waiting for news in front of the compound and their wedding photo and that photo of them where he was wearing a beret and she was wearing boots and they are walking their dog and the photo of him in a tux and her on his lap. On the television all day every day every day.

Gloria could not help but think of him on the bottom of the ocean, thinking about the fishes eating him because while he was terrestrial royalty such a distinction surely is not sub-aquatically reciprocal, wondering further what kinds of fishes were eating him and are they the sorts of fishes that nibble and eat at a strictly cellular level or are they the sorts of fishes who chomp – the fishes you see in those books about aquatic life, translucent self-illuminating prehistoric fish with large teeth and eyeballs that are tethered to their fish heads by long sinewy strands of fish antennae. Or had some other parasite laid claim to him and to them? Like some sort of self-adhesive corrosive algae substance like the barnacles on the bottom of a boat or the mold that eats away at the books in his grandmother's basement? Had one giant organism – like a starfish maybe – adhered itself to him and to her and to her and lay claim to every ounce of each or were they being devoured by millions of itsy bitsy little carnivorous quasi-prehistoric undersea organisms?

They are part of the food chain now, she thought. And regardless of what would consume them, what sort of sophistication the species possessed or what sort of teeth it had or what stage in the evolution of amoeba to reptile to human being it was in during this post-Mesozoic information age, he was wondering what they look like. Down there. Is that sick? Was she sick? Was she a sociopath? Had she been in love with him this whole time? Had the fish eaten his face? Or did they instinctively gnaw on more fleshy parts of him – had they eaten his thighs and belly calves and then proceeded to gnaw on his face and her breasts and her thighs and her buttocks? Did these sub-aquatic carnivores they have some sort of inkling that they are gnawing on one of the most beautiful people in the world? Did the fish now believe that all humans looked like he did and like she did? Will they be disappointed the next time a trio of homo sapiens meets the same fate?

Her mind had been wandering like this since she heard their plane had gone missing; trying to distinguish between how much of her sadness was the result of her unique history with him and how much of her sadness was the result of the inherent sadness of the story; she wondered if she should be ashamed for thinking some of the grotesque thoughts that she had. Was she some sort for hypothesizing on the state of his subaquatic corpse? Then she realized if she was a sociopath she would be apathetic about the whole thing – would keep flipping channels until she arrived at "I Love Lucy" reruns. No. This was more akin to when well-meaning people tell someone not to be sad at the funeral of a grandparent. They mean well but you just can't help it. Or someone inviting you to not think about elephants. You just can't not think about elephants.

Gloria and Ruth Have No Answers

"So wait," asked Ruth, "is his story just over?"
"I guess." Gloria replied.
"That's it. That's how the story ends."
"Yeah."

"Does Gloria Winegar have any sort of responsibility to keep his story going? Like there's more to his story than people know. And by people, I mean the world."

"Gloria Winegar has no fucking clue what Gloria Winegar should and should not do, must or must not do, could or could not do. Gloria Winegar just wants coffee," said a still-dazed Gloria Winegar as she and Ruth walked to the restaurant.

"I've never had someone I slept with die before."

"Me neither. I don't think. He was the last one though. It's odd. It's like when Lucille Ball died, I understood the sadness, but it's not like she was a contemporary of ours ya know? Like there's going to be a day when singers we listen to, actors we watch, authors we read are going to die with some regularity. Is this when that starts?"

"I fucking hope not. I'm not ready for this."

"But someone somewhere has his DNA." Ruth prodded. "Like is this a *Jurassic Park* sort of scenario? Like do we have a responsibility to gather and preserve his DNA in amber? So in case future generations need him they can make him?"

"That's more of a *Terminator 2: Judgment Day* scenario it sounds like." Gloria countered.

"You know what I mean."

"Yeah. I know what you mean. And again. I don't know."

"Have you told Arun?"

"Not yet."

"Maybe you should."

"I will. Imminently it feels like."

"Cool. Let's have some wine."

Gary M. Almeter

Dunkin Donut Love

Arun had been sleeping over at Gloria's with some regularity; and she at his. He began accompanying her to Homer for holidays. Her parents had grandchildren by this point so Gloria's marital status had become less of a topic of concern and so they had fun when they went home.

Gloria enjoyed a new nonchalance from being on the cusp of forty. While her parents liked Arun, what people thought of him was not important. At all. He was also tall and intelligent and had his own house in College Hill. What she liked most about him was that he could make her laugh with ease. And he could laugh at himself. Silly things like the time he confused Clint Eastwood and Burt Reynolds. She also liked his sense of justice; his research; the stories he told of growing up in New Delhi; and that was always doing nice things for people; like the time they were in Dunkin Donuts and they both got large coffees and he also ordered a croissant sandwich with bacon and gave it to the homeless man sitting outside the door of the Dunkin Donuts. On one of their first dates he gave the doggy bag to a homeless man as they walked past him after dinner. He didn't even acknowledge it nor did Gloria get the sense that he was looking for some sort of acknowledgment. He just did it. It's rare to find someone who can instinctually do that sort of thing.

When she took him to Homer, he helped out in the kitchen. A conversation between him and Connie, over a pot of steaming corn on the cob, went something like this:

"What do you put on the corn, Mrs. Winegar?"

"What do you mean?"

"What would you like me to put on the corn?"

"Um. The butter is already on the table," she said pointing to an oblong Tupperware container filled with several iterations of butter sticks, demarcated with corn kernel marks, corn silk hairs, and general decay.

"So just butter?"

"Well now what else would you put on corn, dear?"

"We usually.... well wait. Let me show you." She backed away as Arun found some chili powder and a lime; some cilantro they brought from his garden; and some chaat masala he had brought his hosts as a gift.

And that was the day that Arun introduced the citizens of Homer to something besides butter and salt on corn on the cob.

Celebration

Prior to his proposal, Gloria told him about the time she was impregnated by John Kennedy Jr. and how he didn't know about it and how she and Ruth, of whom Arun was very fond, put the baby on the steps of an old orphanage. She did not miss a detail; including when she had to wet a tissue to wipe dried semen off the glass magnifier on the microfiche machine. She hadn't rehearsed and she hadn't planned on telling him; and she had done no analysis or research or preparation. She just told him as it just seemed right. Arun was definitely not the sort of guy would go to the *National Enquirer* or some such media thing and tell them the story. Nor would he have left. It feels like things are happening the way they should; the way they were always meant to.

They got married in a house on the New York State's Finger Lakes. They invited their families to join them for a weekend and surprise! They got married. The sun set right behind them on the lake as they said, "I do" and it was perfect. Gloria's parents were elated and her dad was happy that he didn't have to pay for it. He said that about 250 times. It felt good to be able to celebrate. It felt good not to be lonely.

She finally moved out of her first apartment on Benevolent Street and into Arun's house, a few blocks away, a little closer to campus and a little closer to Ruth and Will. She and Arun travelled a lot, turning conferences at which he spoke into weeks-long trips; she had celebrated her 20th anniversary at work, a rare feat in that world, so they made accommodation to suit her absences and schedule. They visited his parents in South Carolina. And whenever they visited her parents, still in the house in which she grew up, her dad still treated her like an eight-year-old asking her if she was hungry or chilly or needed anything. She loved being there and she loved leaving, which might sound awful, but she only loved leaving because she loved being home with Arun, loved the life she had in Providence.

They would have no kids. So she celebrated her nieces and nephews as each navigated Boy Scouts and Girl Scouts and soccer and clarinet and football and baseball and piano and volleyball and golf; as they defied expectations and read the whole Harry Potter series and sold magazines to raise money for band trips and sporting equipment.

She thought of her son on what would have been his 21st birthday and hoped he wasn't binge drinking. She had heard a story about a boy who was so drunk he passed out in the snow in front of his frat house and died of hypothermia on his birthday and she was glad her son was born in September. "A few tequila shots are fine," she thought. She wondered if he had good friends. She wondered if he went to college. She wondered if he was in a fraternity. She had lived in the Brown bubble for so long. Did every kid go to college these days? She wondered if he was smart. She wondered what he looked like. She assumed he was beautiful. Maybe he didn't go to college. Maybe he was out on his father's boat catching fish; or in the mill; or in the mines; or driving a tractor trailer truck somewhere; maybe he was snoozing at a truck stop.

Lump

She was at an age where her friends and colleagues used words like metabolism and mammogram in conversation and when she went to the doctor, a friend of Will's, they found a lump and she had a mastectomy and Arun was there and people brought them pies and flowers and balloons and she learned how to knit and made blankets and replicated the zig zag patterned Afghans her grandmother used to make. At some point during all the discussions of her medical history she had to tell someone that she had a baby in September 1983. She told the nurse she gave him up for adoption. And she said "Good for you."

"What does that mean? Like I was going to be a shitty mom?"

"No. That takes courage."

She walked outside and breathed and reveled in the sunshine and she took medical leave and she caught up on books she had always wanted to read but never did – like *The Bell Jar* and *An American Tragedy,* which she had never read despite her familiarity with Chester Gillette. She and Arun stayed in a colleague's house on Cape Cod, in Wellfleet; the colleague's son was on the U.S. Water Polo team and was in Beijing for the summer. Her parents visited them and Arun cooked and ever since Corngate, dinners were very exciting for everyone. And even though Arun was very particular about the way his coriander and turmeric and ginger and garam marsala were all ground, he let Connie ground them.

And whenever someone felt pity, she said, "Seriously dude, if you are going to need a mastectomy, getting it in a city with a hospital run by ivy league educated doctors is not the worst place to be."

Digitization

As the years went by the John Hay Library simultaneously changed and stayed the same. They converted and digitized and uploaded all the microfiche and microfilm so that an eager historian could access it from anywhere so long as they had internet access. Gloria's job evolved into more acquisitions and long-term planning and negotiating data storage rates and she taught some classes on research and referencing and acknowledging primary sources.

She and Ruth still got together every September 12 at a restaurant in Providence's Little Italy where they would reminisce and laugh; and recount the highlights of their midnight ride to the orphanage, like two lady Paul Reveres, two Revolutionary War reenactors reenacting the greatest ride of their lives.

The stories grew just a little taller each year: Gloria's Datsun travelling just a little bit faster each year; the nuns at the orphanage growing a little more menacing with each retelling; did they just walk out of the hospital or had a team of highly aggressive post-natal nurses been on their tail? They thought the latter. And Ruth had the getaway car revving in the Emergency Room loop typically reserved for ambulances. And Ruth peeled away before Gloria had even closed the door.

And Gloria's pain diminished a little bit each year.

One year they decided to reenact the drive for real. Ruth had stopped working but Will's Range Rover still had parking garage access. The hospital had been remodeled a couple times but the general layout remained the same. Providence had grown and become busier and taller but the drive to Fall River had remained the same. The orphanage was now condos though a few nuns still lived there also; all the nun documents had surely been destroyed though. The CVS still sold Pringles.

Ted Kennedy died, and Gloria watched the funeral on TV. The library had removed the microfiche machines years ago and they were employing work study students to digitize all the collections and put them on the worldwide web. Gloria and Arun travelled to India and Europe but enjoyed walks around Providence just as much.

She realized that all her past decades' ruminations and postulations served the dual purpose of satisfying her natural curiosity while also providing a connection to him. She figured that, if he had his father's looks, he'd be married. She figured that his parents had likely told him that he was adopted. That a marriage requires disclosure of family histories and propensities for genetic abnormalities and all that. They likely told him much sooner, people talked about this stuff now – family histories and infertility and mental health. Maybe he was just a foot taller than everyone else in his family. While Gloria was no longer lonely, the realization that she and her son would likely never meet began to dawn on her. And it hurt.

Like really hurt.

PART 3

SANDWICH

Gobble Gobble

He was the center of attention that Thanksgiving 1983 amongst a phalanx of aunts, uncles, cousins, grandparents, who, even though they, as extended Irish Catholic families do, had done this what seemed like a million times before, marveled at a new baby's dexterity and eating prowess and sleeping prowess and general overarching prowess, made the same remarks with the same zest and enthusiasm they had done so many times before. This was kind of a big deal. Patrick and Rosemary Kirby had waited much longer than nine months for their son, who they named Patrick. His full name was Patrick Patrick Kirby, Jr., or "Jay", and even though they had no idea from whence he came and even though his features were a little swarthier than their collective ruddy complexions and shocking red hair, it was clear that he was going to be loved just as much as all the Kirby family members who had come before him; even though he arrived via a far more circuitous route.

He ate no turkey that day, no stuffing, no mashed potatoes. Uncle Patrick did put a little bit of pumpkin pie on his bottle's nipple just to be a smart ass. And that was ok. No pediatrician could fault Uncle Patrick for doing something like that on a day as glorious and celebratory as this one.

Christmas was similarly chaotic and similarly celebratory. His parents, both schoolteachers, dressed him up in a little mini Santa suit and took him to Jordan Marsh for a Christmas photo. On the way back to their home they stopped for a drink and agreed it was the happiest they had ever been. There was a deluge of "Baby's 1st Christmas" Christmas tree ornaments. No one knew, nor could they have known, as they sliced their ham and drank eggnog and exchanged stories about Christmas baking and lines at the mall and lists and cookies and snowfall and Patriots and Celtics and Bruins, that a portrait of the new baby's paternal grandfather hung over the dining room table. Next to a wedding photo of James Patrick Kirby, Sr.'s parents, a photo of Pope John XXIII, and a photo of Patrick Sr., who went by Patrick, and his sisters.

His parents, Patrick and Rosemary, didn't know it when they dressed him up like a little leprechaun for St. Patrick's Day, but their baby was 25% Irish.

One Year

By the time September 1984 arrived he had taken his first steps and had a vocabulary of about fifty words, a favorite toy (a stuffed teddy bear), a favorite song ("Rainbow Connection" by the Muppets), and several teeth. He loved the ocean and going for stroller rides and his mom, a music teacher, singing to him.

His mom was pregnant, with twins, and the chaos never really subsided for a couple decades. They decided to celebrate his birthday on the day they brought him home, September 23, and had a big party to celebrate. As soon as the twins arrived, James Jr. would no longer be considered a baby.

He was spared the usual preoccupation with who he looked like and whose nose he had and whose toes he had and whose hair. If anyone thought that he looked like a more refined though rounder version of Jacqueline Kennedy's father Black Jack Bouvier no one said anything. They may have commented on his pronounced cheekbones and wide-set eyes and dark features and overarching handsomeness; same way they never commented on how he might have looked like a grandmother in Homer, NY with her wavy hair and dimples and twinkly eyes and exuberant expressions.

Coming Around Again

One day in 1987 the Kirbys all went to see Carly Simon sing on Martha's Vineyard. Rosemary worked with a guy who was doing the sound or who knew one of the guys in Carly's band and he got them tickets or passes or whatever it was so they all got to go. His dad held new baby Andrew in one of those baby-holding contraptions that parents attach to themselves to hold their babies. Twins Ryan and Rusty, now three, had fallen asleep in their double stroller - probably the last time they used that double stroller since they were clearly growing out of it. Jay was sticky from having just eaten a popsicle of some sort; you know how kids eat frozen treats at concerts on the Vineyard in the summer and get popsicle residue all over themselves. Rosemary picked him up and squeezed him and held him while Carly sang her "Coming Around Again/Itsy Bitsy Spider" mash up.

From that day on, Jay's measure of love was how close whatever he was feeling came to the feeling of when his mom took him to a Carly Simon concert, let him eat a popsicle and then picked him up without being prompted and squeezed and swayed with him while Carly sang Itsy Bitsy Spider.

He knew he was loved.

Personal History Narrative

They raised him in a small town on Cape Cod – one of the first such towns after you cross the Sagamore bridge from Massachusetts mainland onto the Cape. A town called Sandwich. A kid can't help but love growing up in a town called Sandwich and perpetually manufacturing the circumstances under which the town got its name. How English settlers arrived with pieces of deli meats and cheeses between bread and handing them to the Wampanoags who, astonished by their deliciousness, decided to name the spot on which they stood after the creation.

He often cited his first memory as the day his parents took him to this park in Sandwich, near the Cape Cod canal. The town or the municipality or whatever it is had just paved all those portions of the park which could be paved with crushed shells. It was cold enough that he was wearing denim coveralls because he remembered running with his hand in the pockets of his Hickory striped overalls – possibly his favorite garment that he had ever worn, partially because his paternal grandmother made the overalls and partially because they were just awesome - and blue Converse All Stars. As he ran, ahead of his father, who was pushing the twins in a double stroller and having difficulty because while the shell paving was aesthetically pleasing it was not very conducive to pushing double strollers, he listened to the sound of his Converse on the stuffed shells and thought at the time it was the most beautiful sound he had ever heard. His mom walked behind him because she was at least 8 months pregnant with his little brother.

Slapshot

They told him that they adopted him when he turned twelve. By that time he was already taller than both his parents and his swarthy complexion was inexplicable, amongst a family where five of its six members had bright red hair, freckles, and skin that got sunburned if they stood exposed to the light in the refrigerator for too long. Patrick and Rosemary told him the whole story, that the two of them, at the behest of their parish priest, Father Ridley, drove to an orphanage in Fall River, MA one summer morning and drove home with him. They hadn't even had a car seat. He was already 50% certain of this from watching enough ABC Afterschool specials, each one geared to one of the panoply problems teens might experience. He was more stunned by the fact that orphanages, like the one they described in Fall River, MA still existed, for despite their prevalence in kids' movies and books, who has really ever been to an orphanage? He had to that point thought they only existed in the mind of Charles Dickens and whoever wrote the musical "Annie" and Anne of Green Gables and most of Roald Dahl's books.

The way his father initially told him was comforting. It was neither a grand pronouncement nor intended to change life as they knew it. They, devout Bruins fans and self-pronounced hockey family, were playing hockey on the driveway of their Cape Cod home. Patrick was taking slap shots on his father, who stood in goal with a catcher's mask and bicycle helmet and a Boston metropolitan area phone book tied around each shin and several pillows tied around his torso and legs with twine, in the driveway, standing in a goal in front of their one car garage that they used only for bikes and tents and croquet sets and lawn chairs and beach accoutrements and hockey sticks and lawn accoutrements and terra cotta pots and potting soil and ant killer and helmets of every kind. Patrick shot the pucks at his father as hard as he could and his dad stopped a good number of them. During a break to pick up the errant hockey pucks, they had both remarked on how the yellow twine closely matched the yellow of the yellow jerseys of their beloved Bruins. His father had said, "Some of the best things in life are accidents."

"Like me."

"What do you mean?"

"Dad, I think I know that I'm adopted."

"Wha wha …." He stammered.

"It's ok Dad. I get it."

"Yeah. You're not an idiot."

And then the dad went in the house, invited Rosemary to come outside and toegether they explained.

He rested his hand and chin on the top of his hockey stick, which was resting on his foot, and said, "Yep. We drove to an orphanage in Fall River and pickled [sic] you up when you were about four days old."

"You pickled me up?" and Patrick laughed and said "Yeah. We pickled you up." Then he stopped, exhaled. At this point when he exhaled he expelled so much hot breath which turned to steam the instant it came out of his mouth that Patrick lost sight of him for a moment. Jay took off his bicycle helmet and as Patrick saw the was steam coming off Jay's head, he was certain that he had never loved anyone or anything as much as he loved Jay, the arbitrary way Jay wended his way into their home, his vulnerability, his sensitivity, his strength, and not just because New England winters were cold and he had steam coming off his head, it was all of the prior twelve years hittig him in one stupid ordinary moment.

He continued, "I just want you to know we love you more than anything."

"Thanks Dad. Love you too."

And that was it. He put his helmet back on and Patrick kept slapping slap shots at him. They went inside for dinner, had Patrick looked he would have seen the dad shoot the mom a glance teeming with urgency, and there was never any mention of Patrick being adopted again.

Tying phone books and pillows around his father, their breath visible in the New England cold underneath the fluorescent light on the top of their garage, remained one of Patrick's best memories for the rest of his life.

His father was a high school English teacher. His mother was a music teacher at an elementary school on the Cape and these parents ended up are about as great as they come. They had a three-bedroom house which meant that Andrew and Jay shared a room. They all went to the local elementary school and then to high school at a place called Boston College High School where Patrick was an English teacher.

Green Corduroy

When he was in 9th grade he wanted a pair of cords and a sweater from the Gap for Christmas. Christmas 1998. He had been in high school for a few months and was starting to become very aware and very sensitive and very concerned about what he wore. Partially because such concern was developmentally appropriate; and partially because it was becoming clear that looking good was important in school and with girls and in life. They were at the Gap in the mall in Hyannis when he saw a pair of corduroys and a sweater that he really liked but were too expensive; at least too expensive for a kid who was the son of two teachers and who had three brothers who also wanted all of their Christmas stuff and who would likely be outgrowing them in months and who would be stuffing the clothes into ice rink lockers and in giant gym bags where they would be sharing space with smelly hockey pads and who would be falling down and tearing holes.

The cords were a dark green —like the color of Christmas tree. The sweater was an off-white wool cable knit tennis sweater. He liked them but forgot about them when his mother told him they couldn't afford them. The Christmas morning he opened up the cords and sweater was one of the happiest days of his life. There's tis unspoken rule about Christmas that a gift recipient does not inquire about logistics or budgets or splurges. One just says thank you. So he said thank you; and wore those green cords and sweater until they nearly fell apart; they were as tight as spandex when he finally took them off for the last time and when his mother told him to put them in the hand-me down bin, he didn't. And they remain in a box underneath his bed, along with his old hockey jerseys and graduation cap and a stack of his grandpa's handkerchiefs.

Maybe his kids will wear it someday, maybe his wife will make a quilt out of it someday. Or maybe they will both just sit there.

Imagination

While daydreaming, Jay would often manufacture the circumstances under which he was placed for adoption. At first, he was nonchalant about the whole thing. Then grateful. Then a tad angry. Confused. In biology class, they learned about blue eyes and brown eyes and the nature versus nurture debate and his biological parents took on a different, more multi-layered hue. He'd imagined them as the prom queen high school cheerleader type who got pregnant by the captain of the football team and whose parents forced the adoption; he'd imagined them as the single woman who drank too much at the Legion Hall and woke up in some stranger's apartment that smelled like fish and mildew and so she called her friend to come get her and when she asked "where you are you" she said "I have no idea" and so she started walking and then found a payphone from which she was able to give her friend a precise address and she came to get her and they went to Burger King because she, as hung over as she had ever been, needed greasy croissant breakfast sandwiches and then five weeks later she missed her period and so she went to a CVS and got a pregnancy test kit and sure enough she was pregnant and then was like "oh fuck" and she did not know what to do but all those days of Catholic school convinced her that abortion was wrong so she had him and gave him to the orphanage and then whenever people asked her who the father was she said something like "I'd rather not say" or something like that rather than say "I have no fucking clue" and so there he was. He'd imagined his mother as a nun deflowered by a parish priest; a child; a scared housewife; a waitress; a construction worker; a prostitute; an ambitious finance type woman who did not want her career derailed by an infant; college freshmen who couldn't handle that sort of thing but who are now married with children and who rarely thought of him. He watched cars filled with vacationers go over the Sagamore bridge and wonder if any of the silhouetted heads he saw were the silhouetted heads of his parents.

Watching the cars, the top of each strapped with a rooftop luggage carrier chock full of luggage filled with all sorts of linen and moisture wicking swimwear and Nantucket red shorts and madras plaid shirts and Lily Pulitzer skirts and shorts embroidered with lobsters, along with every possible combination of all that indicia of imminent outdoor mirth, the kayaks and the bicycles and the camping equipment and the golf clubs. So much mirth traveling over that bridge every day. The bridge was often where the people rolled down their windows so they could, after spending hours on I-95, finally get that first big rush of ocean air. Their dogs would stick their heads out of the windows. When the sun hit the cars just right he could get more details on its passengers. Dads typically drove; moms typically sat in the passenger side; kids, having exhausted the amusements of the travel games manufactured by mom – games like "I Spy" and find the license plates and guessing colors and the games mom bought for the trip – games like travel Connect 4 and travel bingo and travel checkers and travel Othello with their magnetic checker pieces - of the were typically splayed all about the cabin: feet on windows and heads on laps and siblings seated as far apart from each other on the back row as physics might allow.

Gary M. Almeter

Water Wizz

When his biological father died he was working at an amusement park called Water Wizz. He was just a little bit late for work on the morning of July 16, 1999 but for the next week, bridge traffic in both directions was unpredictable as media news outlets in vans with big satellite dishes on top and ordinary spectators in regular cars drove to Hyannis Port to watch and witness and pray and spectate and report.

Jay knew who JFK, Jr. was because a couple years prior he had hurt his shoulder playing hockey and the physical therapist who he had to visit twice a week for two months had a subscription to George magazine. The cover with Cindy Crawford dressed as George Washington struck him as funny and whimsical. Had he thought about it he would have decided that he liked JFK, Jr. There was also always a somber feeling associated with November 22. Everyone in the family has some sort of story – the time cousin Ralph was a caddy for Jack and Secretary of Defense Robert McNamara; the time Aunt Peggy was on a small plane flying from Nantucket to Hyannis Port and saw and smelled Ethel eating tuna right out of the can; the time his grandma sat next to Rose Kennedy in church; the time Jackie Onassis was on the ferry to the Vineyard with them; the time that some of Robert's kids cursed when his grandpa was buying a newspaper and grandpa told them not to curse; the time Eunice inadvertently cut her grandmother off in traffic (inadvertently because she was in a blue convertible and her scarf had blown over her face while she was turning right onto Craigville Beach Road) and felt so bad that she stopped in the

173

middle of the road and apologized and invited his grandmother to lunch and insisted his grandmother join her and so she did and Eunice whipped up Classic Nicoise salads for the both of them in about 4 minutes; the time that his dad called Ted Kennedy's office to alert him to some malfeasance happening during the construction of the Sandwich pier and when he called Ted Kennedy answered the phone himself; and then that time when cousin Douglas needed a recommendation to go to the Air Force Academy and they asked Ted Kennedy and he wrote one right away.

He had never lived in another state so didn't know how it was elsewhere, but he suspected that since people are all the same and in light of the fact that people inhabit the states then the way states generally tend to celebrate themselves and revel in their own uniqueness is pretty much universal. He suspected that Illinoisians loved Michael Jordan and Abraham Lincoln and families sat around and told stories about how their ancestors drove carriages for Lincoln and saw one of the Lincolns buying an apple while wearing a soiled overcoat; and he suspected people in New Jersey loved Bruce Springsteen and had stories of seeing him at the grocery store; and Georgians had their Jimmy Carter tales; and so on and so on.

Maybe being adopted put you in a perpetual state of wonderment; maybe you were always hypothesizing about who your family was and who your family might be and where you came from and what sort of chromosomes you might have. Working at Water Wizz had a similar effect. Jay sat at the top of a water slide and every six seconds or so, let the next person down. It was a job for manufacturing stories. How much can you tell about a person from just a bathing suit and a haircut?

And maybe a necklace and earrings? And tattoo? Or tattoos? Who are these people when they are not riding a water slide? What do their falls and winters and springs look like? What do their homes look like? When they go to work is it in an office, a cubicle, a boat, an assembly line, a quarry?

S'Mores

Patrick and Rosemary Kirby lived in that time when social mores suggested that people keep their problems to themselves and that certain topics were strictly off limits. When they got married, at age 20 and 21 respectively, in 1973 they both expected and were expected to have babies right away. But they didn't. Rosemary started to get nervous that something was wrong after about four years of non-pregnancy; anxiety exacerbated friends and relatives, bouncing their own babies up and down on their knees while Rosemary made whiskey sours, when she and Patrick were going to start having kids.

They had been trying since their wedding night.

It was around then that they started to talk about adoption and the first conversations made it clear they had no idea where to begin so they set up a meeting with Father Ridley because they needed someone to talk to and when you are Irish and Catholic and need some guidance you talk to a priest. So whether Father Ridley had some personal connection to this orphanage in Fall River or whether he called someone at the diocese in Boston or whether he just happened to be friends with a nun at the orphanage no one knows and since Father Ridley died shortly after he baptized Andrew, no one will know.

The family dynamics could be best observed during breakfast; and the cadence and chaos of their morning routine – the perfectly choreographed five showers every morning, the smell of coffee, the uniqueness of everyone's breakfast. Jay liked the cinnamon pop tarts; Rusty had Cheerios; Ryan had oatmeal; and Andrew had Eggo waffles with syrup. The parents subsisted on coffee and toast. Then the boys rode with the dad to BC High each morning.

Jay had a penchant for cinnamon-flavored things. For things with cinnamon and nutmeg. And ginger. And Maple. He liked things like carrot cake, eggnog, pumpkin pie, molasses cookies, gingerbread, custard, maple cake, oatmeal cookies.

Brothers

His brother Ryan was on the same hockey team as he was and once, during a scrimmage, Jay on one team and Ryan on the other, Jay checked him into the boards – admittedly hard but not so hard as be actionable and Ryan turned around and just started wailing on Jay. They had each other's helmets off and were both just beating the shit out of the other.

There was a look Ryan gave him – Jay saw the look for a millisecond during a glance at his face in between punches and a look given through clenched teeth and blood flying out of his nose and sweat and spit flying everywhere along with the steam literally coming off of his sweaty head – and it was a look that said, "I want to kill you." It's a look that happens when people fight. Coach skated up to them after what was probably only about twenty or thirty seconds and tore them apart. Amidst a cacophony of "knock it offs." and "hey nows" Coach said, "Come on, you're brothers." To which Ryan replied, "He's not my real brother."

Ryan had it tough, sandwiched between Jay, about six inches taller and frankly, a bit smarter and better looking and way better at hockey; and his twin brother, identical to Ryan except completely different than Ryan and Jay – a sensitive sort of type who wrote poetry and listened to Phish and was really into nature and Greenpeace and animals.

During a frank talk after the hockey practice fight, Ryan apologized. And told Jay, through tears, that sometimes he feared that there is nothing that makes him unique. Jay sympathized but often couldn't help but think about that look whenever he and Ryan argued and couldn't help but think that Ryan's look contained an extra tinge of something that must dwell in the heart of a sibling of an adoptee. He looked like he could have killed him.

Jay had read *A Separate Peace* by John Knowles and fancied himself well-versed in the turmoil and envy and secret animosities that happen and germinate and blossom between young men. And how those animosities and secret hatreds, if not addressed, turn into something very very corrosive.

Commuting

One thing that seemed like a drag at the time but which would, when he was on his proverbial deathbed, definitely be one of the greatest gifts that a person could ever get, was how he rode to and from school with his dad who drove a Jeep Cherokee, uncharacteristically red, with a vanity plate that said "BREZZA," the Italian word for breeze. It was uncharacteristic for Patrick, Sr. to do anything vain. But when you are in Rome you sometimes have to do what the Romans do and everyone in Sandwich has vanity plates. Not everyone but sometimes it feels like it.

For one year it was just Jay and his dad, at the time it was a drag – Patrick filling silences with inane conversation about school and since he taught at Jay's school he knew everything and everyone. And Patrick was very inquisitive. When he asked how Jay's day was, he would not accept "good" or "fine" as an adequate response. And for every question he asked, he had at least four follow-up questions. And he shared all the stories from his own childhood. They would stay with grandpa and grandma whenever it was too snowy to drive home. They both kept a change of clothes in the trunk in case of an emergency like snow. Patrick tried to tell Jay about sex and awkwardly tried to explain intercourse until Jay spared him and said, "Dad I already know all this stuff." They usually ended up talking about music on these 90-minute car rides. Patrick tried to pretend he knew what was hot and what was cool whenever a song cane on the radio; or played his music, what he referred to as classic rock, and quizzed Jay on that. Patrick also quizzed Jay on all things English-related. They also talked about current events and Jay's brothers and before we got out of the car – at school at the start of a day and at home towards the end of one - he always told Jay how proud he was of him.

For three years it was Dad, Jay, Ryan and Rusty. Jay was elated when Ryan and Rusty joined them because it meant that the intensity and the frequency of dad's questioning decreased by 66%. And it was just fun having Ryan and Rusty with them. They took turns sitting in the front seat. They loosened up a bit and dad began to get a little bit more gossipy with regard to which teachers he liked and which teachers he didn't; which administrators he liked and which administrators he didn't care for – though he never put it in those terms. When Jay turned sixteen, Patrick let him drive. Usually on the way home so they could take side roads and not have to worry about getting to school on time. Ryan and Rusty would be in the back set making crash sounds. During hockey season, Dad and Rusty would wait for Ryan and Jay to finish practice. Which added about two hours to their day.

For four years Jay complained about this. The drive was so long and being stuck in an enclosed place – literally incarcerated – with his father for all those hours seemed so oppressive. He just wanted to be normal and to walk home with a friend and play Xbox for an additional hour. It didn't occur to him until he was a father that maybe his dad would have preferred to be by himself also. He was the one who taught all day, got pestered by administrators and hounded by students and he likely would have liked to listen to his music (Pink Floyd, Zeppelin, David Bowie, Genesis) loudly and not have to think or entertain or enlighten an unappreciative 16-year-old.

One of Jay's proudest moments was when his dad asked him how his day was, and he replied, "It was interesting to say the least."

"Oh really? Why's that?"

"I read on the bathroom stall today that you licked Shakespeare's balls."

And his dad laughed so hard he turned red. Jay enjoyed making him laugh. Though his dad made it clear once he regained his composure that he wanted Jay to inform someone on the custodial staff about the graffiti.

During summers, to make extra money, his father worked with a guy who made and installed life-sized chess boards for people on Cape Cod and the Islands. This guy – Harold – made one set a year and had a waiting list. The year that Jay joined them he charged $150,000 for the set. The whole process took about a year, he identified trees in Vermont and then arranged for his Vermont guy to cut them down and deliver them to his shop outside of Falmouth; he spent the whole winter cutting and carving and sanding and polishing and painting. Then in May, he and Mr. Kirby worked together to flatten out the spot and pour the concrete and paint the squares and deliver the chess pieces. Jay helped them paint the pieces, he started on weekends in January and finished them by May. Once someone wanted Red Sox themed chess players and Yankees themed chess players and Harold said no.

Gary M. Almeter

A Few Words about the Word 'Swarthy'

As so frequently happens in families, arguments about one thing have a tendency to evolve or devolve or otherwise metastasize into another thing. One Saturday evening, when he was a senior in high school, Jay arrived home late; twenty full minutes after his midnight curfew.

"Why are you late?"

"I'm twenty minutes late, dad. Relax."

"Relax? OK. I will relax as soon as you can provide a reason why you either can't tell time or decided not to listen to me tonight."

"A car broke down in the bridge dad and traffic was backed up for miles. That is why we are late. It has nothing to do with me telling time or listening to you. But I am so sorry that someone I never met before didn't get his oil changed when he should have and his car broke down and made me twenty minutes, 1200 whole seconds, late."

"Enough with the attitude, Jay. I am allowed to ask where you were."

"Fine. Ask me where I was. But don't accuse me of shit I didn't do."

"Have you been drinking?"

"Yes dad. We had a few beers at Kevin's house. His parents were there and made sure no one drove."

"Oh ok. Again with the excuses. Is anything ever your fault?"

"Plenty is my fault. Just ask mom."

"What's that supposed to mean?"

"The other day we were in Stop N Shop and mom ran into some teaching friend of hers and as she was pointing us all out she pointed at me and said, 'and that swarthy fellow over there is my oldest son James Jr..'"

"Ok?"

"And why the fuck do I have to be swarthy all the time? I get it. I'm different. I look different. But guess what else? Anyone would look swarthy next to all of you Richie Cunningham looking motherfuckers." He said this shouting through tears. Maybe it was the beers. Maybe it was just always there.

"Shhhh. I understand son. I'm here." Patrick said, hugging him. "Let's just go to sleep."

And they went upstairs. After Jay peed and brushed his teeth he went into his room to find his parents sitting on his bed. Rosemary apologized. "You know how much we love you right, Jay?"

"Yeah mom."

"We're doing this for the first time too. We've never had kids before. You're the first. You're our guinea pig. We are going to make some zillion mistakes."

And that was the end of that. And they never called him swarthy again.

And Jay had the sort of parents who could apologize.

Boston College

After high school he went to Boston College where he majored in English, met people from around the world, and before graduation, met the woman he would eventually marry. She had her initials "CRF" embroidered on her backpack and he asked what the initials stand for. She replied with a smirk, "Cecilia Rose Forester." She was from Baltimore and also an English major and their first date was at Fenway Park when the Orioles played the Red Sox.

He had always wanted to go to law school. He was almost 11 when OJ Simpson happened and watched the white Bronco chase and was disappointed he was unable to watch Michael Jordan in the NBA playoffs that evening. Then no one talked about anything but OJ and his trial for a few years and then Timothy McVeigh happened and then his mom started to watch *Ally McBeal* and then Enron happened and all of a sudden he wanted to be lawyer. He didn't particularly like to argue but a hockey coach told him once that he was good at strategizing and predicting. Though he did not like playing chess. Some people from BC who were also planning on going to law school majored in chemistry and engineering so that they would be especially well-versed in areas of technology since that is likely where the money will be in the upcoming decades. But he decided on English. The idea of pacing in front of a jury box with his hands behind his back as he delivered an eloquent closing argument really appealed to him.

Ryan and Rusty came to visit him a couple weekends. Ryan always got drunk; Rusty always ended up talking to the guy at the party with dreadlocks and not wearing a fleece vest.

His parents always made a big deal about birthdays and on his 19th birthday, the whole family ate at a place called Vinny Testa's. He brought Cecilia for everyone to meet. They took the T back to BC and he told her that he was adopted and they kissed, garlic breath and all.

He wondered if he deserved such happiness. Parents, brothers, girlfriend. Education, intellect, height, good looks. He was one lucky motherfucker. He wondered what his biological parents were doing. Perhaps his birthday was nary a blip on their radar screen he thought. Perhaps they were so strung out on heroin for the entirety of the pregnancy that they didn't even know they were pregnant. Maybe she didn't even recall giving birth. Maybe they were dead. Victim to the rusty needles and overdoses and bad batches of the heroin. Maybe they were homeless and do not have access to a calendar. Maybe they did remember. Maybe it was a horrible day for them prompting memories of parents kicking them out of their respective homes and telling them that they never wanted to see you again because of the shame brought on the families.

Jay and his mother always went to a movie on or near her birthday. Just the two of them. She loved the more independent films and one rainy afternoon when he was in 8th grade, and doing a report on Vietnam, he asked her about it. Rosemary had an older brother who died in Vietnam. The next day she came home with a copy of the *Deerhunter*. And that is what started their tradition, one of his favorites. She picked a movie and just the two of them went go. They usually drove to Boston and Jay always had to pay for the tickets and made a big deal about paying and they always stopped for some sort of dessert on the way home.

Cecilia

He liked everything about her: all the standard stuff like her boobs and her butt and her eyes (pale blue) and her hair (short and dirty blonde and perpetually wind swept) and her freckles and the sinewy way her neck met her collar bone and the way she didn't paint her toenails and the way she walked (confidently but still care free) and the way she talked (with a tone that cultivated enthusiasm for whatever it was about which she was talking) and the way she looked at him when they talked and the eyes, flawlessly synchronized and acting in concert with the voice with the hint of Baltimore accent which he had never known existed (the Baltimore accent, not Baltimore) and the sparing way she accessorized and her teeth and her nose. "You know who she looks like?" he told his dad one day, "Is that actress Laura Linney. She played that attorney in the movie *Primal Fear* and was in a movie that mom and he had went to see called *You Can Count on Me*."

"Sounds like a looker."

"Yeah she is."

When he told her that he was adopted she barely paused before saying, "So it is possible that you might be descended from that Russian family that had hemophilia."

"You mean the Romanovs?"

"That rolled rather easily off your tongue. Goddamn it. You're a Romanov! You're Russian royalty!"

"Maybe. I could also be an Osmond, a Von Trapp, a Van Halen, a Beach Boy, or an Oasis brother. Let me sing a song for you to find out." And her started to sing "Sixteen Going on Seventeen" from Rodgers and Hammerstein's *Sound of Music* and she put her mouth on his to make him stop.

"A simple DNA test could determine if you're a Romanov, Osmond, Von Trapp, Van Halen, Wilson, or Gallagher; you know that right?"

"You know whose son I am? Is the lead singer from Aerosmith, what's his name?"

"Steven Tyler" she said, bemused.

"Steven Tyler. Surely he's fathered scores of children about which no one knows. All around Boston. In the early 1980s? Man that guy could get anyone he wanted." And he started to sing, "Love in an Elevator" and again she put her hand over his mouth.

His best friend, Kevin Curran, a journalism major at Fordham, came to visit him one weekend. They met day one, freshman year at B.C. High and hit it off. Kevin was a cartoonist who had had a regular cartoon in the student newspaper in high school which generally made fun of the administration or some aspect of it. It was always in good fun – until the one time he drew a cartoon of Father McCready which sort of overly emphasized the gin blossoms on his nose. And the flask everyone knew he carried around in his tweed sport coat. And the way his hands shook until about 11 a.m. when he had consumed enough gin to make his D.T.'s go away. Kevin was suspended from the student newspaper for two weeks. Kevin's parents thought it was great. They lived in Jamaica Plain, a neighborhood in Boston noteworthy for the progressive attitudes of its population. Both of Kevin's parents went to Harvard; and never married. His dad also went to Harvard Law School and worked at a mid-sized firm where he made about 1/8 of what he could be making if he worked at a big firm. His firm specialized in helping wind energy companies handle and expedite their zoning issues or something. They went to get something to eat. As familiar as Boston was for both of them, to be able to roam around without a curfew, Kevin hadn't even told his parents he was coming to Boston.

Kevin met Cecilia and liked her. The comingling of the two, the intersection of hitherto different worlds, the seamless integration of the two worlds made Jay wonder if he had found the one.

Finding the one was not on his agenda. But even saying the words "the one" prompted additional thoughts. He never had any plans to locate his biological parents, but what if whomever he married needed to know familial health history? Wasn't that a thing people did? When they had this conversation a few years ago, his parents said they would help him find whomever or whatever he needed to identify, especially in light of all that we are learning about genetics. As good as it would be to know from whence he came, not knowing was a huge luxury. He told himself that they were still together and flourishing in their post give-the-baby-up-for-adoption lives. He had the luxury of the possibility – albeit a remote one – that his mom and/or dad might be an ambassador or a Nobel prize winning chemist or archaeologist or astronomer or mathematician. His dad might be Steven Spielberg or yeah, one of the members of Aerosmith, or Gordie Howe or Emilio Estevez or anyone from the cast of *The Outsiders* really or Larry Bird or George Lucas or David Letterman or Dave the guy who founded Wendy's or Harrison Ford. His mother could be J.K. Rowling or Chris Evert or Katie Couric or Ruth Bader Ginsburg or Carrie Fisher or Brooke Shields or Madonna or even one of the ladies from Bananarama!

But he knew that the chances of this were remote. People want to be way more important than they really are. But so are the chances of winning the lottery and people still buy lottery tickets every day.

And because the chances of this were so remote, from time to time he thought about his parents residing on the other end of the cosmic continuum, maybe they were itinerant farmers or coal miners. Or they worked at that plastic molding manufacturing plant or cashier at the Stop & Shop. Maybe they worked at the DMV or the county hospital or the bank or that old timey village in Western Massachusetts where every day they churned butter or replicated the blacksmith experience and sweat their assed off in their bonnets and leather blacksmithing aprons. Maybe they worked at the Wal-Mart and then the new upscale furniture company opened shop in their town trying to capitalize on the influx of city people city buying summer homes in their town so they quit Wal Mart and got a job at the upscale furniture place and they got a job weathering the

Adirondack chairs or hammering the tin that goes on the embossed consoles and buffets they sell. But then business slowed down and they had to go back to Wal Mart and they were happy Wal Mart welcomed them back but then they saw a smirk on your old manager's face when he said, "I saved your apron and name tag" and thought he tossed them the apron and name tag with a little bit too much fervor. They've likely taken side jobs driving wheel chair bound people to their dialysis appointments and building porches and installing invisible fences and painting the interiors of office buildings after 5:00 p.m. and they get to the job site right at 5:00 p.m. and start laying drop cloths on and around the furniture in the lobby and when the office people leave they do not look at them but if they ever did they would look at them with annoyance. During the holidays, they worked at the mall and helped off load Christmas trees because their friend's uncle's neighbor cuts them down from his farm in Vermont and drives almost right through your town to take them to New York City. They have thought about flipping houses but where do you even get the money for that sort of thing even though Jerry who they worked with at Wal Mart did it with that money he got when his aunt died and he bought that old place just off Route 23 or 57 or 168 (that house up the hill) for $78K and sold it for $399K to a hedge fund guy and the hedge fund guy has even kept him around to build some stables and meanwhile they were at Wal Mart and cleaning up the remnants of the jar of Vlasic pickles that someone just dropped in aisle 14. His dad would have loved to coach his son's high school football team, but his work schedule is sufficiently erratic so as to prohibit such things. And sometimes he probably felt that the son was perfectly OK if he didn't coach as the football team is peppered with the sons of doctors and dentists and insurance executives and owners of funeral homes and vice presidents of banks and there's even one guy who commutes into Boston and he drives an Audi and his son is on the football team and there would also be the son of that writer who writes books of which they had never heard but people talked about him like he was some sort of genius and his son was on the football team and what if he was the coach and the writer confronted him with allegations that he was giving his son less playing time or otherwise subjecting him to some sort of injustice and he would likely use a word he did not know while he was excoriating you, some word like infringement or transgression or bereft and then what would he do?

They might be drug addicts and still living at home with their own parents, his biological grandparents. They might work three jobs just to make ends meet. They might have a debilitating disease as the result of where they worked. Like black lung. Perhaps Jay was what prompted whatever downward trajectory upon which they found themselves. He was – after all – the unwanted symptom of a quick romp in a high school friend's parents' room or basement while their schoolmates did keg stands and everyone promised to beat the rival team in next week's football game. What had their team been – the Panthers or the Blue Devils or the Knights or the Crusaders or the Red Raiders or the Corn Huskers? That's it – you were something about corn. The Huskers or the Shuckers or the Jerkers or maybe just even the Kernels.

Or maybe they were doing just fine. They made a mistake sometime in late 1982 or early 1983. But it was autumn or snowy and they were in high school and their football team had

190

in fact just won the state sectional semi-finals and they, enamored with that John Cougar Mellencamp song "Jack and Diane" and the idea of teenage love made them decide to do it and things got out of hand and they had made him but they had the wherewithal to go through with the pregnancy and the birth and then they had the fortitude and character and selflessness to give him to the nuns to find a good home for him. And that sort of intellectual and spiritual and emotional wherewithal suggested to him that they were ok and would always be ok.

Were they Republicans? People who double-dipped nacho chips? People who were perpetually tardy? Narcissistic? Soup slurping? Knuckle crackling? People who borrow pens and then chew on the cap? People who clip their toenails on public transportation? People who crackle their bags of Twizzlers or Reese's Pieces too loudly at the movies? The guy at the gym who dries his pubes with the public hair dryer by the sink or the girl who wears too much perfume or the guy who wears too much cologne?

What would such a reunion look like? His parents had some documents, that they had shown Jay, that literally just acknowledge that they picked him up from an orphanage. Someone had dropped him off there the same way they might have dropped clothes off at the dry cleaner. And they said the nun told them that the nuns found him on the steps. They let the nuns keep the basket and blanket in which he arrived.

Parents

His mom and dad had a long weekend in Vermont and on their way home, stopped to see him. They brought a bunch of apples and maple sugar and asked if her wanted to get dinner. He said sure and asked if Cecilia and could she come along. They went to Vinny Testa's again and Jay barely spoke the entire meal. He could tell if his mom liked someone because after meeting someone she either politely resumed dining or mingling or eating or cocktail partying or she peppered the person she just met with about a thousand questions. Like a hyper-adept defense attorney cross examining the state's star witness mixed with Jane Goodall-esque anthropological curiosity in an effort to know every single cognizable thing there is to know about a person. In the course of two hours his mother asked: Do you have siblings? (Cecilia did. She had three younger brothers, 15, 14 and 10, all of whom played lacrosse.) What are their names? (Anthony, Joseph and Francis.) What made her become an English major? (She liked to read.) What is her favorite book? (To Kill a Mockingbird.) What other schools did she apply to? (Villanova, University of Maryland, Fordham, Bucknell, and Holy Cross. She got into all of them except Bucknell.) His mom loved her necklace and where did she get it? (Which was particularly probative in light of his mom's lack of affinity for jewelry, but Cecilia's necklace was a graduation gift.) Did she live in the city of Baltimore or just outside? (Just outside.) Had she ever been to Camden yards? (She had. And is huge Orioles fan but had a great time with Jay at Fenway which might be her favorite ballpark.) What other ballparks had she been to? (She'd been to Cleveland and Philadelphia.) What did her your father do? (He worked in sales for a company that made stage curtains for theaters and high schools.) What were the curtains made out of? (Lots of stuff.) Did her mother work? (Yes. She worked as a secretary at a school in Baltimore.) Could she maybe someday show them how to eat crabs? (Cecilia would be delighted to show Jay's parents how to eat crabs.) How did she like Boston? (So far so good but Cecilia had not yet survived a Boston winter.) Had she ever been here before? (Just to look at colleges.) Had she ever been to the Cape? (No, she had not but she had heard that it is beautiful.) Maybe she could come visit sometime. To which Cecilia replied that she would love that and to which Jay replied, "Mom that's not a question." To which his mom replied, "Very funny Trebek." Did Baltimore have a little Italy? (Yes. They did. And would she like to come visit sometime? To which Jay's mom replied that she would love to as her maiden name is Giordano and she had a particular affinity for Italian food.)

Thing is. Cecilia was just as adept in her anthropological research. It was tough to discern which one was the anthropologist and which one was the chimpanzee: Where did you get those earrings, Mrs. Kirby? (They were her grandmother's and please call me Rosemary.) Did she have siblings? (His mom was the middle child with an older brother and a younger sister and a brother who died in Vietnam.) Did she always want to be a teacher? (Yes. And she loved every minute of her job.) Where did they meet? (They met at BC. Though not in their freshman year. This is where his dad piped in and did his schtick about how he and Jay's mom literally met at church and then talked about their classmates who spouse swapped after spending their entire four years together.) Did they leave Ryan, Rusty and Andrew by themselves this weekend? (No. Their aunt stayed with them.) Did she love lobster? (Absolutely.) Had she ever had Maryland crabs? (No.) Did they go to Vermont every fall? (Yes. But usually earlier than this but they had a wedding to go to on the Cape the weekend they usually go in October.) Are they skiers? (Yes.) Had they ever been to Baltimore? (They went to a wedding there once in the late 1970's; before Camden Yards and before Cal Ripken, Jr. and before the National Aquarium so feel like they haven't been there.) What sort of day was it when they drove to the orphanage to pick Jay up? (It was sunny. "A perfect day from start to finish." Jay interjected.) What a pretty sweater. (Thanks.) At which point Jay told Cecilia that his mom made the sweater herself.

Jay and his dad were content, scooping the gelatinous garlic cloves from the baked bulb and spreading it onto the bread.

During the meal Jay also learned that Cecilia liked to knit and that one of her brothers played lacrosse with Cal Ripken, Jr.'s son and that her father and her mother went to New York City once a year for a show at Carnegie Hall (usually a piano concert) because when Cecilia's dad was coordinating the installation of their new curtain he struck up a friendship with the director who now invites them to annual shows and that her mom grew up next to Tom Clancy and his family and that her dad was once an extra on NBC's *Homicide: Life on the Street* and that she won a short story contest at her high school for a short story she wrote about a woman who worked as a bottler at the National Bohemian brewery and lost her class ring in a bottle of beer.

Sometimes Jay felt guilty for the life he was leading when there were so many others – adoptees and putative adoptees and non-adoptees who, he assumed, were sad or hungry or hurting or abused or neglected – who would never eat at Vinny Testa's with their girlfriend and parents. It really was not fair. The aphorism "life isn't fair" was of no comfort. The fact that Father Ridley's fingers flipped through his priestly Rolodex and his fingers landed on Patrick and Rosemary Kirby when he was born – whether it was arbitrary or whether there was some sort of list – made him the luckiest person alive. There is no way that the adoptee prior to him or the adoptee just after him or however they do it got as lucky as he did. And for that he sometimes feels guilty.

Roommate at the ER

His roommate, Whitten, had to go to the ER one night. He came back to the dorm and passed out in bed, woke up in the middle of the night to pee and peed on the floor by his desk and then slipped and fell in his pee and cut his face open on the edge of his desk. Jay woke up when he heard his piss splattering on the floor but didn't really register what happened until he heard Whitten scream. Since Jay was one of the only sober ones in the dorm, he borrowed someone's car and drove Whitten to

St. Elizabeth's hospital where he got eight stitches in the side of his head. Whitten and Jay, for the first time ever it seemed, got brunch when Whitten woke up. While Jay thought he was being kind of a baby as hockey players got stitches all the time, Jay had fourteen in his left calf once after this kid Brian fell and his skate sliced through his hockey pants. When they were about done with brunch Whitten said, "Can we just hang out here today, Jay? I need someone to talk to and I doubt my other friends are really up for it." and they spent the whole day in the cafeteria just talking. While it would be breach of loyalty to divulge what they talked about, Jay was learning that the people who we think have it all together were generally the ones who have it the least together.

Walking back to the dorm, Whitten thanked Jay for taking care of him.

"You're one of those inherently likable people, Jay."

"What the fuck are you talking about?"

"You are just the sort of person people like. You're lucky."

"Thanks. But whatever dude. I think you busted your head harder than we thought."

"No. I mean it."

"Whitten you're the one who's gone every weekend visiting friends in high places."

"That's different."

"Look Whit, I am not 'that guy' who feigns ignorance or fake modesty. I'm proud of who I am. Which is not easy for a Catholic to do. When someone congratulates me for some hockey thing or some academic thing or paid me a compliment, I typically say 'Thank you.' I'm good with acknowledging my talents. I didn't give the talents to myself. But I am also just not a guy to whom people are typically drawn."

"You'd be surprised Jay. You're more of leader than you realize."

"I was never in student government in high school or anything."

"Big fucking deal."

Something happens when men open up to each other. He is the last guy he would ever expect to reveal a weakness or flaw. And he did. He liked his authenticity.

Pregnancy

Someone down the hall confided to Jay that his girlfriend was pregnant and they are still talking about what to do but they are both leaning towards aborting it. Wow. Heavy stuff.

Union Oyster House

One Saturday, he and Cecilia walked around Boston. They had New England clam chowder at Union Oyster House and just sat and talked and then took the red line to Harvard and walked around Harvard and their football team was playing Yale and that was a huge deal and they pretended they were smart as they talked at this place Grendel's Den and then they took the bus back to Brighton and ate dinner at this place called Sunset Grill and Cecilia got a cranberry flavored beer and Jay got a pumpkin spice flavored beer so it was like thanksgiving. They found a bakery with pumpkin muffins and they split one and then she said, "I love you" and then he said "I love you too" and then they took the C train back to Cleveland Circle and they made out on the T and did not care who saw them and what they might have thought.

Giving Thanks

He went home for Thanksgiving. He felt like a rock star meeting his dad at his old high school on the Wednesday before. Some folks from the English department were waiting with his dad and all hugged him when he walked in. They were having a few beers so they were probably a little more excited than they should have been. He felt great driving home with Ryan and Rusty. And now Andrew. Like no time had elapsed. But he could tell they held him in just little bit higher esteem than they used to on all those ordinary weekdays. Andrew's unique perspective made the ride more interesting. Ryan and Rusty's college applications were all done and submitted. Ryan wanted to play Division 1 hockey and had applied to Holy

Cross, Colgate, Cornell, UVM, UNH and Rusty wanted to be a writer and applied to Middlebury, Harvard, Columbia, Fordham, and NYU.

He had forgotten how great the ocean air smelled in Sandwich. And how small their kitchen was. And how great it was having unlimited ham and cheese in the refrigerator. Perpetual ham and cheese that he could just eat whenever he wanted. His mom got him a pint of Ben & Jerry's Cookie Dough ice cream when she was at the grocery store ("along with every other idiot in Massachusetts apparently" she said) as a welcome home gift and he would eat whole thing by himself that night after he watched a movie. He liked letting it sit on the counter for about 45 minutes until it reached the perfect consistency.

Cecilia texted him to let him know she got home safely.

The next day they did Thanksgiving: mom cooked all morning and cleaned and rearranged furniture and got the good forks and the good china from wherever it was that she stored it and she made a list of things to do like get ice for the beer and put it in the tub outside and wiping folding chairs that had been in the basement since last Thanksgiving and then people started coming over and the house got so crowded until people found their spots in front of the TV or in front of the stove and then they ate a meal which lasted about 10 minutes and then there was discussion about when to have dessert and there was a faction of people who went back to watching TV and a faction of people who washed dishes and a faction of people who went for a walk and a faction of people who went outside to play football. There was an uncle who smoked and an uncle who drank too much and became a boisterous jovial drunk for a few glorious minutes until he became a belligerent drunk and talked to his wife and kids just a little too tersely and just a little bit too aggressively to make everyone wonder what happened when family was *not* there and it was *not* Thanksgiving and they also had an aunt who drank too much but who tried to hide it by drinking wine or vodka out of a coffee mug but she would start to slur her speech sufficiently to make everyone wonder what her life was like when family was *not* there and it was *not* Thanksgiving but Thanksgiving was not the time to talk about that and inevitably they will talk about politics and it would soon become apparent that if these people were not his family then he likely would not hang out with them that often but he loved them anyway because that was everything he ever knew.

Christmas

He made Cecilia's Christmas gift that year. He made a star stencil from the cardboard of the Sam Adams 12 pack the Collinses brought them for Thanksgiving – a star about six inches wide from farthest point to farthest point. Then he took the star stencil and traced it twice on spots large enough on his favorite green corduroy pants. Then he cut out the stars and sewed them together. Yes, he did this all himself. Then he took some cotton stuffing his mom had and stuffed the star. It was sort of a pain making the stuffing reach the ends of the points but he persevered. Then he sewed the remaining edge but not before he added a yellow and maroon (Boston College colors) ribbon to make the star an ornament.

He did this all on the dining room table where everyone could see him and they asked him what he was doing and he told them and they laughed and he did not care that everyone knew that he was in love.

He lent his abortion friend $100. The $100 his drunk uncle gave him to take Cecilia out to dinner. He was still processing his thoughts on abortion. But when he was talking to his friend he saw fear; and he could only imagine what she is feeling. Were they stupid? Perhaps? Are they human? Yes. Are we all human? Yes. Are there lots of ways to respect life? Yes. And this whole fetus business is just one of them. So he felt ok with this.

When all is said and done, he thought, everyone is just doing the best they can.

And when all was said and done again, he was certain that the man and the woman were just doing the best they could do also.

PART 4

BREWERS HAVEN ISLAND

Letitia Wingfield

Jay met Letitia "Tish" Wingfield in the summer of 2008, when he was a second-year law student at Boston College Law School, working at a firm at Ropes & Gray in Boston. All summer associates worked for a week or two in all the practice areas in which they might have interest in working upon graduation and Jay settled on and into the Private Client group when he began working as an associate in September 2009, a month after the bar exam. He and Cecilia were married by this point and she was pregnant. Lucy and Lillian Kirby were born during a snowstorm in January 2010. Melody followed in 2012.

One of Jay's first clients was the Wingfield family, who had been firm clients for generations. Then they became his biggest client. Soon they were his only client.

Tish had invited Jay to leave the firm and join the Wingfield pay roll. For big stuff – mergers and acquisitions and international sort of stuff, the Wingfields would still use partners at Ropes and Gray but they liked Jay and had enough daily stuff – daily wealth management issues and real estate concerns and cease and desist orders for nosy tourists for a full-time general counsel. Tish was the great great great great great great granddaughter of Edward Wingfield, who accompanied his cousin Bartholomew Gosnold on one of the first British trips to the colonies. They landed in Maine then wended their way down the coast to Virginia where Bartholomew Gosnold eventually established a settlement. Along the way, however, Edward Wingfield fell in love with the daughter of a Massasoit leader, married her, and stayed in Massachusetts where they raised their family. The family owned a number of the Elizabeth Islands, off the coast of Massachusetts and maintained a family estate on Brewers Haven Island. Brewers Haven Island appeared on some maps; but Tish's dad had called J. Edgar Hoover or Robert McNamara or Caspar Weinberger and the Wingfields had a permanent injunction on any photographs being taken or any satellite imagery being obtained of any of the islands upon which the Wingfields dwelled.

Jay and Cecilia were on their way to Brewers Haven Island to meet Tish; Cecilia needed some convincing that leaving the firm – the firm that had been so generous with Jay with the salary and the paternity leave – and joining the Wingfields full time. The whole thing just sounded risky, sure, but also insanely not risky. And when something seemed too good to be true....

Tish was eager to welcome them onto the island, their family island, though her island if everyone wanted to be completely honest with themselves. She was the one who maintained it and made decisions regarding the buildings; she was the one who used the main house as her main residence. So of course she would be there as the helicopter descended to give them an embrace and a welcome and cocktail. Jay told her that Cecilia was very fond of her Rosemary Palomas but, rather than risk being a bit too obsequious, Tish greeted them with

Bourbon Rickeys. It was September; after Labor Day but still warm enough so that summer cocktails were appropriate. And besides, how could Cecilia really say no to the opportunity she was offering Jay?

If Letitia were going to be completely honest with herself, she would say that she found him attractive, that she was likely a – what was the term the hoi polloi was using these days? – oh yes, cougar. But he was young enough to be her grandson. She was 86, a young 86 despite a face weathered by mountain sun and beach sun and ocean sun and dessert sun and mountain wind and beach wind and ocean wind and dessert wind. All the sun and all the wind had participated in weathering Tish's face; and Tish had felt and loved it all.

With the clout he knew he had, Jay made it clear to Tish that this was a recruiting trip. That Cecilia had reservations. So Tish was to be indomitable, indomitably charming and indomitably engaging and indomitably witty, when it came to convincing his wife that working for exclusively for the Wingfields was a good career move. Jay made it clear to her that he wanted the job but his acceptance of it was contingent on Cecilia's OK. That was fair.

Tish realized at an early age that she would never find anyone like her beloved father and having witnessed some of the turmoil her friends had gone through and having realized that she valued her independence far far too much, she had never married. But she understood that these sorts of negotiations were part of the ordinary course of business in any marital union. She was surprisingly nervous. She surrounded herself with the best and was accustomed to getting as much. And she considered Jay the best. There was an ease with which

Jay carried himself that made her want to be in his atmosphere. She knew anyone could navigate the trust laws sufficiently to maintain their wealth. Whether they earned *x million* dollars per year in interest or *x+10 million* dollars per year was really of no consequence to the generational wealth they had amassed in the 400 plus years they had been trading and shipping and buying and selling and generally amassing.

Jay wondered if he was teetering on disloyalty to Cecilia with the efforts and orchestrations he undertook to make sure things went well for this meet and greet. Disloyal was too strong a word and conspiratorial was too criminal. It was sneaky. But not traitorous. Seditious might be the best word. He told her she wanted the job and while she would have acquiesced to most anything her affirmative buy-in would help matters considerably. A job such as this – being on constant call, last-minute travel requirements, an odd blend of Tom Hagen-esque consigliere with the law stuff for which he went to school, would upend their status quo.

Tish knew Jay was adopted though wasn't sure if he had told her or if they had learned that during the process of vetting him for the role of personal trust attorney. A sizable portion of her time was spent devoted to matters concerning or ancillary to lineage. She loved discussing the nuances of genetic derivation and identifying the progenitors of those with whom she dealt. Because no one had better progenitors that she did. Those conversations wherein she pulled out her litany of ancestral triumphs – a great uncle Henry who had married a Vanderbilt niece and a great aunt Esther who married a Carnegie nephew and a grandmother who travelled to Paris with the Frick daughters and a great great grandfather who boarded with Rockefeller's son when they were at Phillips Exeter. It was choreographed. And after eighty some years of it, it had grown tiresome. It is spectacular, these things that people do with their lives. But how many times can you talk about wealth before it stops giving you goose bumps? And there were also the times they vacationed with the von Bulows and that time her brother dated Leona Helmsley. So you have to balance these things, she learned.

Dinners and meetings and organizations and philanthropic endeavors were peppered with those who really did nothing to "earn" the seat at the table. But what does it even mean to "earn" something or to "deserve" something? It seemed to her that if people got what they "deserved" then most people – herself included – would be dead. How many times did she cruise around the Hudson valley in the two-seater of some Yale or West Point or Harvard student whose blood alcohol content was well above the legal limit? How many times had he crossed the yellow line in his little two-seater convertible? And had the audacity to sip gin from a flask while so doing? So she knew that she was lucky; that she hadn't earned what she had; and that those who thought they did - all of those people with whom she was schooled and with whom she summered - were fooling themselves. So she really cared less about pedigree than she let on in those arenas where pedigree was lauded. She was similarly proud that, despite her free-wheeling demeanor, she had restrained herself from ever asking another member of society about whether they thought their whole existence was a fiction.

The political climate of the day also lent itself to a renewed emphasis on what was deserved. Boomers yelling about how millennials think that they deserve jobs and conservatives yelling about how illegals think they are entitled to their low-wage jobs. People telling everyone else to stop whining. People telling other classes that no one owes them anything. That rather than bitching about whatever situation in which they find themselves, they should have made choices. Better choices? Letitia had never really ever made a choice that would have altered her destiny in the slightest. What choices? Stop being lazy? Working for years to get enough money to pay someone to provide access to a train and then walking hundreds of miles north while carrying you child and then hopping onto the roof or a train car and riding that train further north towards that same border while fending off rapists and other parasites while simultaneously making sure your children don't freeze and then hopping off that train when you get to America and then doing whatever it takes to become self-sufficient – did not sound lazy to Letitia.

She differed with her friends in this regard. She knew it was a luxury. Tax rates and credit shelter trusts and capital gains taxes and whatever the fuck else they had to pay made nary a blip on the Wingfield financial radar screen. So the fact that someone could save her a few million dollars interested her not in the least. She was more concerned with character and kindness.

And at this stage in her relationship with Jay – and to be certain, it was a relationship – it was just one of those things that you know about a person as though inherently, like the way you know how your spouse likes his or her iced tea or a sibling doesn't care for mayonnaise. It just was. Every now and again, however, she found herself wondering from whence he came.

It hit her once – when she was travelling in Africa in her twenties – that the only difference between her and the individuals who were tasked with carrying her luggage was that she had the good fortune of being born into the family she was. And that was really it. Put people around a fire and invite them to eat by pulling meet off a fresh and freshly barbecued antelope carcass and she soon realized that people are really the same. At least that was her conjecture. Or something in between something she conjectured and knew to be true. Without the encumbrance of a husband she was free to explore and test this hypothesis with some frequency.

What does a person do when they can do anything? When you're Letitia Wingfield, you go to Paris and Shanghai and you do an African safari and then you go to Morocco or you might make Morocco a separate trip and you visit Rome and Sydney and Buenos Aires and then you start to yearn for something more authentic so you go visit Mayan ruins and Aztec ruins and Greek ruins and all of the ruins and then you visit a girlfriend who married someone in the film industry in Los Angeles and when you are in Los Angeles you realize that Americans are just as interesting and just as varied as anyone else and then you decide to drive back to Massachusetts against your mother's wishes but your father understands so he wires you money to buy a car and you buy something plain – something in the Chevrolet family – to drive across the United States and you visit all the places where ordinary people go like the Grand Canyon and the Gateway Arch and Mt. Rushmore and then you realize that humans are really fascinating so you go to bingo halls and chicken barbecues put on by volunteer firemen who want to raise $3800 over the next two years to buy a new firetruck and that really strikes you because the emerald brooch your mom has also cost three times that much and she never wears it and how is that even fair when something that just graces one woman's lapel could, if spent differently, change a whole town.

Island

The islands on which Tish and her family lived, the islands they owned, sat like kneecaps rising just above the surface of bathwater. From overhead, they were perfectly spherical and had a sheen or luster reminiscent of freshly exfoliated and moisturized kneecap epidermis.

As the island on which they would land came into view, it struck Cecilia just how much like a child's concept of what such an island would be, if such a child's kindergarten teacher asked him or her to draw one; or make one with Lego. Half of the island – exactly one half as though the island were split in half through its epicenter - was one half trees. Lush verdant flawlessly green trees – surely many of the same trees that the first people to ever see the island surely saw - which stood in contrast to the other half of the island where several large buildings stood on perfectly manicured grass along with a pool, horse track, tennis courts. Whomever designed the Wingfields' life on the island relied on a finite number of simple shapes and basic polyhedrons; the houses, each covered with monochromatic gray cedar shingles, were large rectangular blocks atop which sat large triangular blocks; the pool, like the tennis courts, were perfectly rectangular, the horse track was a perfect oval, a baseball diamond provided a perfect square. Circumventing all these simple buildings was a coastline peppered with equally basic docks which serviced a series of boats of varying sizes and colors. The array of colors on the boats against the dearth of colors on the island made them look like precious stones glued onto a simple green crown.

Oddly, the Wingfields, in their multi-century history in America, had achieved the rare double victory of a) existing and promulgating uninterruptedly for nine generations; and b) existing and promulgating with nary a scandal or public embarrassment among them. To be sure, there were ancestors who had engaged in episodes evincing moral turpitude, some of them likely might have been considered criminal, but when you dwell on your own island it is easy to keep evidence of moral turpitude to yourself.

Cecilia Is Taken Aback

Tish greeted Jay and Cecilia warmly. One of the Wingfield ladies expressed astonishment that she and Cecilia had never met before – as though not running into Letitia Wingfield at the grocery store or at the dump or at a PTA meeting was inconceivable.

They enjoyed a lovely meal and she got back on the plane for the quick ride back to Hingham, feeling comforted by the fact the Wingfields seemed to truly know and value Jay. She was also comforted by the fact that she identified no evidence of any malfeasance – nothing to suggest that their wealth was the result of decades of child trafficking or colluding with the drug cartels of South America or selling uranium to the North Koreans or anything nefarious like that. She was comforted by this but also secretly a little disappointed. For she left with nothing in her arsenal for the impending discussion regarding whether he should leave the firm to work exclusively with the Wingfields except for a gut feeling which didn't even rise to the level of *bad gut feeling*. It was something more akin to a lingering unidentifiable quasi-malaise lite, hovering somewhere in the ethers above her. Something just felt amiss.

Since graduation, things had been so easy for them. Like the whole thing had been scripted; or choreographed. If she had to think of a problem it was the time they came to a standstill regarding which house to get. In Hingham. And he used the term "my income" for the first time and it was very jarring and she called him on it and he apologized but not in a pathetic way just in that way that Jay did that made him inexplicably both incredibly vulnerable and incredibly omnipotent. And she guessed there was also the time when they were going to Baltimore to spend Christmas with her family and he suggested that they get a motel instead of being cramped with everybody and she remembered the days when he flourished in the chaos of the Forester home; insisting on helping her mom cut onions and bake cookies and playing football with her brothers and their friends and helping her dad string up Christmas lights and while the idea of staying at a hotel in Baltimore over Christmas to avoid the chaos in which he once thrived and (she thought) made merry, was quickly and instantaneously eviscerated once she gave him a look that was part fury and part quizzical and part hurt, the idea that his mind had been capable of forming the thought hurt nonetheless. But that was it. She had been hurt, mildly hurt maybe even just mildly annoyed or just "taken aback," twice in the relationship since its inception. How do you complain when you have known someone for twenty-six years and the only flaw or complaint or sorrow you have experienced is that you have been "taken aback," twice, maybe thrice? That means she gets "taken aback" once every thirteen years or so. She'll take it. She's not washing up on the shores of the Mediterranean while trying to escape Syria or riding the top of a cattle car on a train towards the border of the Mexico-Texas border. Though if given more time she might also identify that time he bought an Audi with his initials as vanity plates. Like it was *his* car. That didn't even hurt either. Nor did it rise to the level of being taken aback. It was just this awareness of a new nuance or idiosyncrasy. So in the course of a relationship that spanned a quarter century, she had been taken aback twice and made aware of a new nuance once. Still not so bad. Especially in light of the fact that so many of their fellow eagles and neighborhood friends were starting to separate and divorce; cheat and get cheated on. Already they had been to two second weddings. Though one was a sixty-something partner at work who married his thirty-year-old girlfriend who didn't really count.

Their lives had been so easy that she found it hard to breathe sometimes. An abrupt exhalation might bring the whole thing down.

They proceeded through Boston College. There was a minor hiccup junior year when she had mentioned that someone was cute and Jay teased her and she teased back and then it escalated until Jay said that maybe they should see other people. They both went on two dates. And Jay had a drunk hook up with a freshman of which she was aware but of which she asked no details. They got back together right before they went home for the summer and at that point they just both sort of knew. Jay got into Boston College's law school. She got a job teaching at Brookline High School. Jay excelled at law school. She loved teaching. They got married in October of his third year – after his summer at Ropes and Gray. Bar exam – no problem. Partnership at Ropes and Gray – no problem. Pregnancy – no problem. Everything was easy. And fun.

She wasn't complaining. But sometimes the momentum grew monotonous; when the status quo just seemed a little bit oppressive. Sometimes the malaise happened when she might ask herself "what's next?" It might be "we are done with Halloween; what's our next holiday?" or "I painted the mud room, what's our next home beautification project?" or "We just got back from Disneyworld. What's our next destination?" but every now and again she asked, "what's next for me and my life and my journey towards fulfillment?" and she realized that that was no *next*. This was it. This was as good as it got. And barring something cataclysmic like some kind of North Atlantic tsunami or one of the America's largest law firms going out of business, there would be no interruptions. They would acquire more things and there would be the thrill of sending daughters to college and watching them *become* – but the rest of their lives was by and large set forth already. But then there were the days when she woke up and told herself, "this just can't last" and the malaise manifested itself as an intense fear of the elimination of the status quo. To say she was unhappy would be a huge overstatement; but to say that days peppered with malaise – either the sort where she lamented the status quo or the sort where she lamented the abrupt demise of the status quo – were becoming more frequent would be accurate. It was tough to distinguish what was unique to her and what was just part of the state of being on the cusp of middle aged and on the cusp of obsolescence with your children being able to tie their own shoes and brush their own teeth and ride their own bikes to their own friends' houses and download their own music on their own iPhones and suddenly not think Cecilia walked on water or knew everything.

Jay's enthusiasm for her and his desire for her had not diminished. Or had not diminished disproportionate to the general wear and tear and erosion and disintegration and attrition and atrophy that happens over time in any relationship, any marriage, any friendship. Like a rock in a stream that gets smoothed and rounded over hundreds of years. It's not bad that the stream rock is now round and smooth; that's just what happens when the forces of nature do what the forces of nature do.

Easy

Before the twins were born they talked about Jay locating his biological birth parents. To see if he was in fact, descended from Czar Nicholas II or some other infamous carrier of maladies or infirmities. After you work at a large law firm for a few months, you realize that anything is possible; that there are pitfalls lurking behind every corner; that statistically speaking, while the sorts of emergencies one might read about are unlikely, they are possible. And they happen to a *someone*. Every accident on the MassPike, every tsunami, every tornado, every boating accident happens to *someone*.

Additionally, being a lawyer teaches you quickly that you can hire anyone to do or say or accomplish or investigate or opine on or determine or establish *anything*. His very first assignment during his first summer at Ropes and Gray was to identify an expert witness who would opine and testify, contrary to the plaintiff's expert witness, that the free will decision making capacity of people was not diminished when they were in crowds. This as Ropes and Gray was defending a concert venue where a 21-year-old plaintiff was rendered quadriplegic when he went mud diving at a Phish concert and broke his neck on a PVC pipe. Jay immediately called Rusty and told him to never go mud diving at Phish concerts and then found an expert at Harvard who would opine that people maintained their free will even at Phish concerts. So he knew that if he wanted to he could hire someone to find out from whom and from whence he came. There was so much data and DNA and digitized records out there. And so many people eager to make a buck. It could be done. No problem. Certainly for less than the cost of the leather seats in a new Audi.

But they decided to play the tape backwards. Even if they had discovered that Jay's grandparents were in fact Czar Nicholas II and their kids would have a 75% chance of hemophilia, would they not have kids? Or what of it was only male offspring and they only had a 50% chance of hemophilia. Would they not have kids then? What if it was something less noxious than hemophilia? Like maybe just a predisposition for smoking? Or gambling? Or deviated septums? Or any of the other minor flaws that can befall homo sapiens.

So in light of the fact that any information they acquired would not really affect their decision to procreate they decided to forego the biological parent identification. Also, a sizable amount of their discourse was spent talking the nature of loyalty and allegiance. Jay was not ashamed to tell Cecilia that he would feel disloyal and guilty if he tried to find his biological parents. Despite the assurances of Patrick and Rosemary that they would not be hurt or offended if he wanted to, he suspected they might be a bit hurt.

Tish Gets Déjà vu

Jay took the job with Tish and her family. He was in his office in the cottage adjacent to the main house where he was completely self-sufficient. Tish was out picking blueberries in the area of the woods behind the main house they referred to as the blueberry bramble. At this point in Jay's employ with the Wingfields, he no longer had to check in or let people know he had arrived. He would talk with Noel the pilot and arrange for Noel the pilot to pick him up at one of their meeting places, typically Buzzards Bay.

From where Tish stood in the blueberry bramble, she could see Jay and she was certain that Jay could not see her. So she watched him for a spell. There was something intriguing about him. She saw it when he had introduced her to his friend and colleague Whitten. And convinced her to let Whitten assist in devising a seeding vehicle strategy for the Wingfields hedge fund. Whitten seemed to be as enamored with Jay as she was. She also saw it in the kindness he showed to his brothers. She knew he was paying for Rusty's apartment in New York while he tried to make a living as a writer. And she knew he paid for his brother Ryan's visit to Hazelton. And a good chunk of Andrew's tuition at SCAD. And vacations for his parents.

Tish watched Jay as he innocuously put a pen in his mouth. Ostensibly people did this to promote thinking but everyone knows this is just a habit. Seeing him do this prompted what people refer to as déjà vu; though hers was maybe something a little stronger than mere déjà vu. She saw his profile against the double glass doors behind him and saw the one the pen dangled from the side of his mouth. It hit her when he removed it with the index and middle fingers of his left hand – he did not do so effeminately but with a flourish that prompted her to think about her dorm mate at Vassar.

Letitia's roommate at Vassar was a total bore – Letitia could scarcely remember her name – likely because she went home to Philadelphia nearly every weekend to spend time with her boyfriend who was in med school at Penn. Letitia, needing someone with whom she could both frolic and raise hell, befriended the young lady two doors down from her on the third floor of Vassar's Main House; a young lady named Jacqueline Bouvier. They were friends that first year. It was rare for women to smoke cigarettes in those days; rarer still for Vassar girls given the unladylike connotations people attached to cigarette smoking. But she and Jackie did so with some frequency.

There was something in the way Jay put the pen to his lips and smiled that prompted Letitia to think about this, it was barely a thought at all. Just an image that crept from her subconscious; a subconscious that had catalogued over eight decades of minutiae. Something resembling something on the cusp of cognizance that Jay held his pen like her friend Jacqueline Bouvier held her cigarette.

Maybe she was wrong about her learned indifference to pedigree. Maybe, she wondered, if that is all people are – just the amalgamation of centuries of ancestral idiosyncrasies and genetic memories. Maybe people ate short ribs the same way the way their great great great great great great great great great great great great grandfathers gnawed on the woolly mammoth carcass *because* of the way those ancestors gnawed on the woolly mammoth carcass. Maybe we could trace a line from our every phobia, anxiety, hang-up, and aversion back to its origin in the experience of a great great great uncle or aunt or grandparent. The way we were frightened of snakes or spiders or sharks or darkness or clowns or suspension bridges was the result of someone else's experience which nestled into some chromosome and got passed down to us. Maybe we like cinnamon and eggnog and green corduroy because someone else did; a someone else from whom we inherited a random chromosome. Maybe we are less responsible for our inclinations and impulses and penchants and overarching temperament than we think. Maybe we are less ourselves that we realize. It's comforting – to know that we can excuse mistakes as the result of some sort of genetic defect. "It's not my defect, I'm just the result of my genes."

But maybe it's also a little discouraging.

Certainly we have the free will to do whatever we wish – but what if the mechanisms and mechanics and protocols or how we execute that free will is all predetermined by the blips and bleeps and protons and neutrons of DNA? What if the chromosomal bleep that made great great great great great great Aunt Dagmar Domgoole laugh like a constipated dragon is the same chromosomal bleep that makes you laugh like a constipated dragon? What if the way you sneeze twice in a row in rapid succession whenever you sneeze is due to some morsel of DNA from another distant ancestor? The way you chew, the way you run your fingers through your hair, the way you pound on your keyboard, the way you tap your foot, the way you run, jump, dance, sing, hop, skip, gallop, the faces you make when you pee, poop, ejaculate, cry, laugh, ponder; the noises you make when you pee, poop, ejaculate, cry, laugh, ponder; your handwriting, your propensity for biting your nails, your predisposition for sunburn and acne and cold sores and canker sores and eczema and ringworm and leprosy and chancres and chickenpox and boils and rashes and lesions of any kind. The way you look at a loved one; the way you drink milk; the way you drink water; the way you drink beer; the way you drink wine; the way you drink vodka; the way you like to roll up your pants? What if the way you like to roll up your pants is some sort of remnant of some pre-Darwinian attribute developed and ingested and seared on to the DNA of some prehistoric grandfather who rolled up the skin of some prehistoric primate that he had tied to his own legs whenever he went hunting and/or gathering?

She laughed at the idea of dragons getting constipated. And wondered if fire came out of their butts when they did. And laughed at the idea of having an aunt named Dagmar Domgoole. And proud of herself for giving herself Viking ancestors. She was proud of herself for thinking outside the box.

But then she got back in the box – back in her blueberry bramble watching Jay Kirby chew his pen - to strategize how to determine if her friend and consigliere Jay was a descendant of her Vassar dorm mate Jackie Bouvier. Strategize is actually the wrong word. Strategize is what generals and those on the cusp of a skirmish might do; she neither wanted nor anticipated a skirmish. She envisioned something more compassionate. Something more benevolent. Like a benevolent blueprint.

They had been so concerned about who Jay did not look like that they had neglected to address who he did look like.

Gale. Her roommate at Vassar was named Gale. Gale Kellogg Drumheiser. She and Jacqueline called her "Stale Humdrumheiser." They lived at 316 Main House at Vassar.

Gary M. Almeter

The Etiquette of DNA Swabbing

The idea of swabbing his DNA from a napkin or water bottle struck her as impossibly tactless so she opted to determine his lineage the old-fashioned way, by hiring a forensic genealogist. She was aware of the old axiom about money not buying happiness and she wholeheartedly concurred. But also wanted – needed – people to know that there was an asterisk at the end of that axiom directing attention to a footnote that identified all the things that money could buy. It would have been a sizable footnote. Several African safaris, an expedition to the North Pole, trips through Europe, lunch with royalty, the Range Rovers, the Porsches, that 1954 Sting Ray her nephew wanted for graduation from Yale, admission to Yale, their name on a building at Yale, their name on a building at Harvard, their name on a building in Washington, D.C. housing some agency or other, that helicopter they used to fly Billy Joel in from Long Island to play piano and sing for an hour at her niece's wedding, that movie she funded in 1989 which afforded her a trip to the Oscars which begat a friendship with Meryl Streep and afforded her the opportunity to enthusiastically and unapologetically slap a certain Best Actor nominee that year for feeling her ass, the necklace she wore to that Oscars, the personal meeting with Carolina Herrera to design a dress for her to wear to those Oscars, the islands they owned, the house in Monaco, the house in Beverly Hills, the ranch on Montana, the 12 full time employees they have at that ranch, the 16 full time employees they have on the island, the ski chalet in Aspen, the buildings in Manhattan, the mountain in the Adirondacks, the plane they used to fly Sinatra to the island to sing for her dad's 75th birthday party, the plane they used to fly Barbra Streisand to the island to sing for her mother's 75th birthday party, the warmth and assurance they received from giving the Diocese of Boston and the Diocese of Fall River all the resources they needed for all the works performed by the Catholic church, *ad infinitum*. To be sure, their lives were not free from worry and episodes of unhappiness but certainly those episodes of happiness were no more momentous than that of any other family. Now, the asterisk would include, top-notch forensic genealogist to discreetly identify your attorney's birth parents because if the one of them is who you think it is then you will have been the catalyst for something important to happen, and that is a feeling which one rarely gets to feel. Gravitas. Is gravitas a feeling?

She lived in a world where there was etiquette for everything, including discreetly contacting a forensic genealogist. She, despite the aura of someone who might be cavalier about some things, adhered to standards of etiquette and decorum.

She contacted the necessary persons, authorized unlimited spending and initiated the protocols for determining who James Patrick Kirby, Jr.'s parents were. It would involve a priest, two bishops (one from Boston and one from Fall River), a nun, several clerks in several municipal file keeping offices, several clerks in several hospitals, a private eye dressed as a priest, that same private eye dressed as a doctor, that same private eye and a former nurse named Ruth.

It was really sort of a bargain.

People are not as expensive as you might think.

Gary M. Almeter

A Good Name for a Private Eye

Samuel Hackman was not his real name. His real name, Howard Zielinski, was far less intimidating than Sam Hackman; certainly not intimidating enough for a private eye. And when he met Tish's brother Frederick, somewhere in Asia, sometime in the 1960s, under circumstances that neither ever talked about, he was in need of a new start and a new name, not because he had hit any sort of rock bottom but because he needed to be hidden for a decade or so. So he hid out as a gardener for the Wingfield family. Then Tish needed him for something – something about sabotaging Alabama Governor George Wallace's 1976 run for president in 1976 – and it turned out he still had his special set of skills.

Sister Leonella Gets a Visitor

Her face had not changed much since September 1983, still nearly perfectly round; still compact and vaguely Nordic; still pinker than most faces to the point of being ruddy. Her general demeanor had not changed much either; still youthful to the point of being spritely; still eschewed many of the tenets of convent life, preferring solitary activities like hiking and watching movies to the daily communal events – the lunches, the dinners, the church pew polishing, the altar floral arranging.

225

On the steps of the convent stood a man. She was leery of men in general. Leerier still of men who showed up unannounced. Leerier still of men who showed up unannounced at convents. So when this man rang the bell of the convent, Sister Leonella answered it slowly and reluctantly and defiantly. Like a child might turn off the TV when told to do so by his parents at bedtime. And for some reason – call it intuition – she knew that the man at the door had nefarious motives. The tone of the doorbell chimes was the same as all of the other times it had chimed, typically limited to the wayward parishioner, trick or treaters, and Christmas carolers, but she was certain that today, the doorbell chimes rang with a more ominous portent.

The man had a weathered look. Like a man who had seen the worst in people and was intimately familiar with fear but whose fear had metastasized into perpetual disgust and perpetual boredom, as though whatever he might encounter could in no way ever cause any sort of alarm or bemusement. He was ill-at-ease in his tan slacks and navy blazer; because it was hot and because neither fit well and because he hated them. His forehead shone with sweat and he was winded just walking up the stairs. Sister Leonella looked him up and down as she unlocked the door and greeted him with as much coldness as someone as warmhearted as Sister Leonella could muster.

"Hello. What can I do for you?"

"Graham Hackman …. M'am…. Or Sister." He said in a friendly, almost lilting voice that belied his gruff exterior.

"Sister is fine Mr. Hackman."

"Sister….."

"Sister Leonella."

"I'm here to speak with someone about a baby boy who might have been left here in or around" he paused here to flip open and sloppily page through a small spiral notebook, ostensibly to review some notes, but it was all for dramatic effect as he had committed to memory precisely when Jay was left there, "the third week of September 1983."

Despite the fact that her residence – her residence for nearly three decades - had the word "orphanage" carved into its portico, finding babies left in baskets underneath was a relatively rare occurrence for Sister Leonella. It had happened only a handful of times in the time she had lived there and never since the building – an enormous red brick orphanage, convent, chapel, and elementary building, a Catholic megaplex of sorts, in the middle of town – was converted into residential apartments. Perhaps leaving babies in baskets with notes pinned to their blankets with safety pins was an antiquated practice. Sister Leonella attributed it to the legalization of abortion, of which she was a staunch foe. She would have eagerly housed basket babies in lieu of them being vacuumed out of the womb. But that's another topic for another day. Anyway, because she was such a staunch advocate for life, she just happened to keep the baskets and blankets and accoutrements of such babies as a testament to her enduring commitment to life.

So she recalled with almost alarming certainty the child of whom Mr. Hackman spoke and knew exactly where she had housed the basket and blanket and general infant accoutrements of this child.

Sister Leonella asked Samuel Hackman why he was inquiring of this particular baby and he produced a card from the Wingfield family. Even Sister Leonella – a nun who reveled in her vow of poverty and shunned the excesses and turmoil and turbulence and extravagances of the modern world – was impressed. And then mildly alarmed. Then even Sister Leonella – a nun who celebrated her commitment to humility and subservience and devotion to the divine – could not help but be intrigued by the notion of being a part of something big. For if the Wingfields of Massachusetts were involved then you know it had to be big. Sister Leonella, seeing the weathered man in a new light, invited him in and offered him lemonade and invited him to sit down as she scurried down into the basement to retrieve the basket and the note and the blanket that was left at the orphanage thirty-five years ago. When she was a novice nun. Like Maria in the *Sound of Music*. So ardent and filled with vigor and reverence and joy. She grabbed everything and scurried back up the stairs.

The man examined the basket, a non-descript multi-purpose shapeless wicker basket; examined the note, a page of notebook paper on which the terse "Please take care of my baby and please find him a good home." Had been written with blue ball point ink; and the blanket, white flannel with teal and fuchsia stripes at its edges and Women & Infants Hospital stamped in one corner. The man asked Sister Leonella if he could keep the blanket to which she replied in the affirmative. And off he went.

Then, just as quickly as her feelings of intrigue and awe arrived, those feelings dissipated. And in their place, she felt shame. For having succumbed to them if even briefly.

Samuel Greets Ruth

She had left her job at the hospital as soon as she learned that she was pregnant. "Why do that to myself?" she thought. "On my feet all day." William made plenty of money. And she took care of their son, tried to have lunch with Gloria once a week. There was a period when they had lunch every day for six straight weeks. One of Gloria's dark periods. One of her, "I am going to be alone" forever periods. Ruth had several various approaches to this. Her instinct was always to (try to) be funny, "You fucked the sexiest man alive. Multiple times. You are not going to get any sympathy from me. Ever." Or she would identify People's sexiest man of the year that year and invite Gloria to find him and fuck him silly since those tend to be the guys who tend to fall for Gloria. Sean Connery in 1989; Patrick Swayze in 1991; 1992 was a rough year so Nick Nolte was referenced with some frequency; as was Pierce Brosnan in 2001. Sometimes that worked. Most times it did not. She would encourage her to go out dancing, go out drinking, join clubs, go to church functions, do karaoke. Later they would explore dating services and online dating. And then she met Arun.

For the better part of the first decade or so they knew each other, Ruth and Gloria just hung out and watched tv. And Ruth held Gloria as she cried. Depression is a nasty motherfucker. Gloria had so much guilt that, when it surfaced, frequently plunged Gloria into a depression. And the guilt was multifaceted. She felt guilty for the whole adoption thing, guilty for lying to her parents, guilty for the resentment she had for her sister who stayed home and did things the normal way and was living a perfectly acceptable life, guilty for fornicating on top of and getting her love making juices on top of an archived document. She felt guilty for selling the car her dad bought her; for not calling her grandparents enough.

With all that said, her friendship with Gloria was never a sacrifice. Most of the time Gloria was fun and adventurous and atypically wise and generous. Ruth considered her an anomaly and told her so with some frequency. In fact, her nickname for her was the "Fuckable Archivist." Because who ever heard of a librarian – an archivist no less, an archivist on the bottom of the librarian food chain – fucking the sexiest man alive? It. Just. Never. Happened. So in that regard, Ruth considered herself fortunate to have Gloria as her best Providence friend. At the every least, it was interesting. And whenever she considered the possibility of forming a modicum of a thought of a notion of a possibility of telling one of her college friends that her Providence friend Gloria had just had JFK Jr.'s baby, it was the inevitableness of losing Gloria's friendship that dissuaded her from so doing.

Ruth wondered if Gloria had some bizarre hope that the three of them (John, Gloria, and baby) would one day meet. As it was the plane crash in July 1999 that really propelled Gloria into a nearly frenetic search for something that would prompt her to start (or resume) living her life. She never *blamed* John Kennedy Jr. for impregnating her nor did she *resent* him for graduating and being sexy and starting a magazine and surreptitiously getting married. It wasn't resentment that kept her single, it was this speck of a germination of an idea that the three of them would somehow be family. Someday. There were times when Ruth often wondered if Gloria might be capable of leaking her own secret. There were days when Gloria, at rock bottom, would say things indicating that she had absolutely nothing to lose if she moved back to Homer and nothing to lose if she stopped going to the gym and nothing to lose if she told professor so and so or asshole ivy league student so and so what they could do with their urgent request for document retrievals, that lead Ruth to believe that Gloria might just tell some news outlet that John Kennedy Junior had a son because what did she have to lose? A little excitement, a little break from the status quo, a little deviation from that which she had planned for the week would do anyone some good. At least make life interesting. Very interesting. Ruth thought it was likely her parents – good corn-fed upstate New York peoples who adhered to and believed in old fashioned things like farmer's almanacs and scarecrows and pumpkin patches and borrowing cups of sugar from your neighbor while you bake a pie crust to set on the windowsill – that prevented her from doing something as cataclysmic as leaking her secret to some news outlet.

Ruth also recalled those weeks following her dad's layoff from the Smith-Corona factory. Which coincided with John Kennedy and Daryl Hannah being in the tabloids for romping around Martha's Vineyard and romping around Manhattan and romping around Hollywood and romping around the Hamptons and just generally chronically romping. Which coincided with her boss getting some sort of promotion. Which created something resembling a perfect storm of disdain for people who had more than she did and who had lives easier than she had and who had life easier than her dad had it; her dad who had worked his ass off for decades to give Gloria all that she needed, which was another period wherein Ruth thought Gloria capable of spilling the beans.

Even when someone indicates that they have nothing to lose they still likely have lots to lose.

Then Arun came. What a spectacular man.

A different man, a grizzled and coarsely complected man in tan slacks and a navy blazer – but not the sort of tan slacks and navy blazer so ubiquitous in a city with an Ivy League university as its epicenter – was standing on her front steps. He rang the doorbell. She answered it. And knew instantly that something was off, he somehow just emanated something sinister. There were no visible prison tattoos or piercings or scars or knife wounds– but he had the look of someone who definitely has prison tattoos and piercings and scars and knife wounds. His clothes were somehow too nice for his face – he had the face of someone who had seen a great deal of sorrow. Someone who would no longer wear nicely pressed khakis and a navy blazer and a blue shirt were he not compelled to do so. And his watch was too nice. And his shoes too shitty. And his belt too belty. And he asked her if her name was Ruth Steward Buckmeyer. She told him it was, and then he asked her, in a tone that she would never forget, a tone that indicated that he already knew the answer to the question he was positing, what she was doing on September 12, 1983.

And it was what she imagined that thing when your life flashes before your eyes might feel like. Except it wasn't her life exactly but her life since it had intersected with Gloria's.

Gary M. Almeter

Briana Brentwood is the Worst Fake Name

Frankly she felt relief. Which is to say that amidst the fear and confusion and anger she was feeling at the moment, she also felt free. In that way that surely people, who in opposition to the Vietnam war would rob banks and inadvertently kill a security guard and never get caught until someone set forth a deathbed confession or a neighbor happened to be watching *America's Unsolved Mysteries* the same day he happened be watering his hydrangeas, felt when the authorities finally showed up and arrested him.

The sinister man identified himself as Sam Hackman, gave her a card identifying his client, Letitia Wingfield, and produced a packet filled with documents – timesheets of the day identifying Ruth's name as someone who had not punched in but who had checked out some vials of painkillers; patient sheets identifying a woman named Briana Brentwood checking into the ER to have a baby but never checking out.

"Briana Brentwood? This is the name you two used?" he asked with amusement.

"Yeah Mr..... what did you say your name was?"

"Hackman."

"Like you're one to talk Mr. Hackman. Yeah, Briana Brentwood. Not the best fake name but we were new to the whole let's sneak into a hospital and have a baby undetected thing. So give us a break."

Then he produced a document with St. Joseph letterhead on it and a statement from some Mother there indicating that she had received the blanket on September 15, 1983 along with a basket and some money. And that through the intervention of Father Ridley of Holy Redeemer parish in Sandwich, MA, she had given the baby to him to be placed with a family in Sandwich, MA.

The man said that the nuns had been eager to talk with him. But his employer had to promise some key hospital personnel a hefty donation before they would become willing – even eager - to let him inspect their files and timesheets and documents kept in the ordinary course and again, it was surprising what people would do for money, even violate HIPAA.

As is so often the case in these sorts of things, the smoking gun is neither smoking nor is it a gun. It is a white flannel baby blanket from Womens and Childrens Hospital, the ones with teal and pink stripes at the edge. He was holding one. And waving it nonchalantly – nonchalantly teetering on menacingly – around. He said that he got from the orphanage in Fall River, who keeps everything for just such a scenario.

Frankly it was also sort of comforting that good old fashioned human ingenuity was still of some value, and that people could still not ever get away with things even before the era of omnipresent security cameras and observational protocols and perpetual and all-encompassing observation.

So Ruth told Sam Hackman everything. Almost everything.

She did not tell him who the father of Gloria's baby was. Gloria could do that.

Gloria did what she did. This was not a betrayal. At all. Of this Ruth was certain. Gloria did what she did and this was the logical result; perhaps the only result.

From her medical ethics class, Ruth recalled the professor postulating about the ethics surrounding organ donation and organ donor lists. And how the way it was supposed to work is that no matter who the person who needed an organ was, they had to keep their place in the list which meant that if the Pope and some unemployed trailer park dweller with a confederate flag tattooed on his bald head both needed a liver and the unemployed trailer park dweller with a confederate flag tattooed on his bald head was one spot in line ahead of the Pope, then that unemployed trailer park dweller with a confederate flag tattooed on his bald head would get the liver first. The idea being that no man's life was worth more than any other man's life. Which everyone seemed to know was a fiction.

Because the life of the man for whom this man was searching was somehow worth more than most others.

A Photo Array

Gloria never told him – this Sam Hackman Wingfield detective person – who the father of her baby was. It was like he intuitively knew. And when he confronted her with it she tried to hide it but then her lip started quivering and she felt a solitary

235

tear roll out of her left eye and down her cheek. Then, without telling her the name of the man in the photograph, he showed her a photograph of Jay. He showed her five photographs – like that photo array thing they do on cop shows when the victim identifies the culprit from looking at five suspects and identifying the one who did it. But this was five photographs. And she was not a victim she was a birth mother. And all of them were of this man who just happened to be the spitting image of John Kennedy, Jr. Though he had Gloria's wide eyes and her dad's nose and it looked like his eyes might twinkle the way her grandmother's did when he smiled.

How did people not catch on or suspect that he was JFK Jr.'s son? That's right. Someone did. And had. And they hired a forensic genealogist to find her. Which he did. And he was standing in hers and Arun's home now.

Goddamn they had made a beautiful child she thought. They should have made more. They should have had a dozen babies. How the past thirty five years would have been different had she had a dozen beautiful little JFK Jr. Jr.s circumnavigating her and pulling on her apron strings as she did her domestic duties then going to bed while she and John went to movie premieres and black tie dinners and let's face it, he would have been in the White House someday and she would have been first fucking lady of the country. All of her sister's boasts about her kids' spelling bees and soccer games and bullshit trophies would have been superfluous. She could have just sat there filing her nails nonchalantly as she listened to her sister drone on about spelling bees and then when and if her sister ever finished she could have – Emery board still in hand – said, "Oh Yeah – just take a good fucking look at my little

236

JFK Jr. babies and shut the fuck up." Oh my. That was hostile. That escalated quickly as they say. But she felt it. She did. She was feeling proud of her child.

And he wasn't such a child anymore. He was a thirty-five-year-old man.

So she wept. Like a lip quivering chest heaving gasping for air splotchy face mucous flinging kind of sobbing. So Sam Hackman, the Wingfields' forensic genealogist, embraced her. He could not recall ever embracing an interviewee before. And he liked that he could still be surprised, even after decades in this business. He held her while she sobbed – decades of sobs – for twenty minutes or so. It felt like hours to him but it felt like mere seconds to her. That is the difference between holding someone who sobs and being the one who is sobbing.

So maybe Sam Hackman was not such a bad guy after all. He had a job to do. And he did it.

And he received the confirmation for which he was hired – albeit implicitly and circuitously – from Gloria Winegar that she is Jay Kirby's mother and John Kennedy Jr. is Jay Kirby's father. Mission accomplished. Everyone knows everything they should and could and wanted to know and no one knows anything that they shouldn't know.

Unless you have ever seen the son you left on the doorstep of a convent in a photograph after surmising and supposing and wondering about him about him for three and a half decades, you will never know what it is like to see that son in a photograph after surmising and supposing and wondering about him about him for three and a half decades.

If you are a parent: you know that feeling you have when you are at a farmer's market or flea market or some sort of outdoor market (it has to be outdoors and you will see why in a minute) and you are looking at, inspecting really, a zucchini or some tomatoes or some basil or whatever you typically buy at a farmer's market or if at a flea market, you are inspecting a stack of old vinyl records from the 1970s, what you consider the apex of music, David Bowie and Pink Floyd and Zeppelin and Rush and Frank Zappa, and while you are inspecting the zucchini or rummaging through the old Queen and Clash albums, you look up to make sure your son or daughter – too big for a stroller but not yet big enough to be off on his or her own – is there and he or she is always there so you get lulled into thinking it's a safe space and then one time you look up from the zucchini or basil or Jethro Tull or Black Sabbath and you realize the son or daughter is not there and for somewhere between 20 and 40 seconds, you are terrified that your child has been abducted and you are frantic and terrified and your heart sinks and your brain feels like someone is pouring hot asphalt into it but then you see your child around the corner – maybe at the jam and homemade jellies stand if at the farmer's market or the vintage Fisher Price toys stand if at a flea market – and you drop the zucchini or the Meatloaf album you were intent on buying and you rush over to him or her and hug and the feeling of franticness and sorrow and fear and terror suddenly dissipates. Recall that feeling when it all dissipates; and then multiply by like twelve or fifteen or maybe even twenty and that is what it is like to see the son you gave up for adoption in a photograph after surmising and supposing and wondering about him about him for three and a half decades. Except you didn't even know you had that feeling of heart sinking and terror and dread because you had just gotten so used to it so the feeling is extra super liberating.

If you are not a parent, the best way she might describe it is if you were really good at tennis in high school or maybe you were in a band in high school and maybe even laid down a few tracks and maybe if you were good at tennis you even had some recruiters from Division I colleges and universities come take a look at you while you played and you loved playing tennis and you loved being in the band but then you just stopped playing tennis because you didn't play in college and there was never enough time and then you gave up playing in the band because everyone went to different colleges and things just were never the same but then one day – you might even be in your thirties at this point with kids of your own who have very disparate interests than yours – and you pick up a tennis racket or bump into one of the band mates at the grocery store (probably over thanksgiving break when everyone comes back to their home towns) and you decide to play music together after you are done cutting the turkey and eating the meal with your respective families. That feeling you get when you hit that first ball and recall the sound the racket strings make how good it feels to hit a cross court winner and to serve an ace or if you were in a band, that feeling you had riding your bike to your band mate's house (we will call him Jimmy) with your instrument (let's say it was a guitar) strapped to your back and then pulling up and hearing your band mate's tuning their instruments except this time you are in your family car, likely a Toyota Sienna or some such thing, and you walk into Jimmy's garage and you plug your guitar into Jimmy's amp and you start to strum and Jimmy has cold beers for you and this time they aren't snuck from Jimmy's father and they aren't cheap like Pabst Blue Ribbon or whatever local cannery Jimmy's dad bought beers, this time they are some sort of IPA brewed from the micro-brewery that just opened in your town. When you hit that first tennis ball or strum that first chord and down that first gulp of locally brewed IPA and realize that you are meeting an old friend again, that is what seeing the son you gave up for adoption in a photograph after surmising and supposing and wondering about him about him for three and a half decades. Except way more than that. Like also play tennis or play your guitar again but while you are doing that your favorite childhood pet, the one that died a few months after you went to college, joins you and if it's a dog then he nuzzles up against you and then rolls over so you can scratch his belly and if it's a cat then maybe the cat acknowledges you. Plus after your tennis match or guitar practice when you reacquaint yourself with your childhood pet you go home and your favorite childhood cereal, the one they had to take off the market because it contained too much sugar and asbestos and lead paint and whatever the fuck else it had in it, is there on the kitchen table waiting for you to pour it into a bowl. And then also a hug from your favorite grandparent and you smell the grandparent's smell – whether its mothballs and old perfumes in his or her sweater or old breath mints or lotions or hairspray or whatever it is, you get to hug the grandparent and smell them again.

That is what seeing the son you gave up for adoption in a photograph after surmising and supposing and wondering about him about him for three and a half decades is almost like.

Metamorphosis

There are a very certain and very few points in a life when a person stops being one thing and instantaneously begins being another. When a judge bangs his or her gavel and a person is suddenly a felon; when the dean says congratulations and a person is stops being a student and becomes an alumnus; when a person has a baby; when you have a wealthy boss who uses any means to find your biological parents and you stop being anonymous.

Of course people choose to emphasize certain things when asked who they are. "Who are you?" Well where to even begin. You're under no obligation to let everyone know you're a felon; or an alumnus; or a parent; or a welder; or doctor.

"Lucy I'm Home"

When a spouse comes home from work – perhaps he or she is even home earlier than normal - and discovers his or her spouse in the kitchen whisking some sort of hollandaise sauce in preparation for dinner or searching for something – batteries or a Chip Clip most likely – in the junk drawer or in the garage repairing a child's video game controller or gluing a ceramic dish back together or outside raking leaves and mowing the lawn and uncharacteristically interrupts and says, "Honey, we need to talk" it is likely that something cataclysmic is nigh; that the status quo is about to be upended; that life as the spouses know it will never be the same.

The Kirbys of Hingham had just that sort of day one day in May 2021. Jay, returning from a day on the Wingfields island, pulled into their driveway in his Honda Pilot same as always. Cecilia would recall later that she was in the kitchen making those spirally French fries with her spiral French fry maker when she saw him get out of the car and she knew that something was amiss the minute she saw his face. At the very least a moment like that will confirm that while life as you know it will soon be upended, when you share a bond like that with someone, the life you have with that person is the life you are *supposed* to be living because bonds like that – where you can tell something is amiss just be looking at someone's face through a kitchen window and across a quarter-acre sized front yard – are rare.

Jay walked in the kitchen and said, "Honey we need to talk." Cecilia, seemingly instinctively, turned off the stove. She left the chicken in the oven because it still had thirty seven more minutes to bake. And she and Jay went to the living room to talk. Lucy and Lily were outside playing; Melody was in the sunroom coloring. Jay told her – she would decide later that he told her too abruptly and she would tease him about this abruptness later – at the outset,

"A few months ago Tish observed me in her study with a pen in my mouth. This reminded her of the way Jackie Bouvier used to smoke at Vassar so she hired someone to find my birth parents and yada yada yada my mother is a librarian in Providence and my father is John Fitzgerald Kennedy, Jr."

Cecilia could not help but focus on the yada yada yada. When did that become part of the lexicon and when did that become an acceptable substitute for actual words and actual insight and actual communication? If she were to guess, she would have said that it happened in that *Seinfeld* episode when Elaine was describing a date she had that started with lobster bisque and yada yada yada her date never called her again. And Jerry said, "you skipped the best part" and she said something about mentioning the lobster bisque. Typically, her husband was not a fan of the compression and diminution of the English language. She recalled once when his brother and he were playing frisbee and the brother (she thinks it was Rusty) threw the frisbee out of the range where Jay could catch it and so Rusty said , "My bad" and then Jay and he had a long discussion about how "my bad" had replaced actual words of genuine contrition and how upsetting that was then pretty soon children would be saying "My B" and then eventually just "My" whenever they threw a frisbee out of catchable range or underthrew a football to a wide open receiver or hit a tennis ball out of reach during warm-ups. So it was really more the yada yada yada that stuck. But then everything else began to register and wend its way through her intellectual digestive system.

But then it was her turn to speak. To respond. To communicate back to him. To make words.

She had always known he was adopted and had always just not cared. Like genuinely not cared. In fact, during a post-engagement get-together – not a formally sanctioned party but just a time when she and Jay and his parents were having dinner – and they were talking about Jay and adoption in general and Jay's adoptedness and she said, "I don't care" and everyone started laughing because it came across as apathetic. And she was not apathetic about Jay. She just could not make herself think that his being adopted was significant. Later that night she took her mental thumbnail and scratched a little beneath the surface of what she was saying. While she was trying to be kind and accepting the idea of saying "I don't care" about a fundamental characteristic of someone she loved, it makes it sound like that characteristic is more of a flaw than a mere characteristic. Like if someone had an unborn twin growing out of the side of their head and you said, "I don't care." She did not perceive Jay's being adopted as a flaw. She was nearly certain of it. And the more she thought about it, it was not necessarily so that when someone said "I don't care" in regard to a partner's characteristic that the characteristic was to be deemed a flaw. Say for instance that someone's boyfriend was really good looking and the partner said, "I don't care about looks." So she assured herself that apathy did not necessarily equate with discounting one's flaws.

He might have told her a zillion other unbelievable things which would have been more believable than what he had just told her. That the United States was at war with Australia; or that some inhabitants of Jupiter had just landed on the front lawn and wanted to talk with her; or that they were visiting Earth because they had heard her pumpkin pie recipe or her New England clam chowder recipe was out of this world; or that the United States was at war with Jupiter; or that they had just won $100,000,000 in the Publisher's Clearinghouse sweepstakes; or that their family had just been chosen to join the United States Olympic Cornhole team even though corn hole isn't even an Olympic sport (yet) and even though they don't really play much corn hole; or that she had been invited to replace Celine Dion when she ends her residency at the Coliseum at Caesar's Palace; that we have scientific proof that Santa Claus has been real all along and he lives at the North Pole and elves make all the toys; that *Jurassic Park* was really a documentary and the dinosaurs are still roaming Isla Nublar; or, if she knew that he was about to reveal his genetic make-up, she probably would have been loss shocked if he had told her that he was a long-lost Von Trapp family singers; or descended from the Ingalls family of "Little House on the Prairie" fame; or his parents were Burt Reynolds and Loni Anderson; or Frank Sinatra and Mia Farrow; or Bob Barker and one of the models on the Price is Right, Janice, Dian or Holly; or Holly Golightly and the unnamed narrator of Truman Capote's "Breakfast at Tiffany's;" or Mork and Mindy; or Sonny and Cher; or Donny and Marie Osmond; or one of the guys in Hall & Oates and one of the ladies from Cagney & Lacey.

Any one of those scenarios would have somehow been a little less shocking than what he just told her. It would take some analysis to fully understand why – though some of it would surely have to do with all those times she had lusted after her now father-in-law. She remembered being in high school in Baltimore and watching his funeral and saying, "Goddamn he was so fucking hot." And her friend telling her she was being disrespectful and her saying that calling someone hot was not disrespectful *in the least* and then the friend saying that it was "the way" she had said it that was disrespectful. And fuck it – she was no longer friends with that high school person anymore anyway. And she would talk to her therapist someday about the time she wanted to fuck her would-be father ion law. Something for a therapist to parse and analyze.

But for a moment – in their living room on a sunny afternoon in May 2021 – she had to decide how to respond to what her husband of ten years had just told her, that he was the son of John Fitzgerald Kennedy, Jr. Which would make him the grandson of JFK and Jacqueline Bouvier Kennedy Onassis, one of the most famous and glamorous and beloved persons who had ever lived. It was like in movies when the people got in an automobile accident and the camera showed it in slow motion with the occupants of the crashing vehicle hair flying all about and them giving each other bewildered quizzical expressions and the glass and the stuffed animals all floating through the air as though they were all on the space station and not in a crashing automobile. When we all know a crash really lasts but like a millisecond. That is what she felt like. She asked herself, "How does one respond to this? Is there etiquette for this?" She read his face and could not tell if he was elated or terrified or mad or sad or happy or glad or proud or embarrassed or apathetic or what in the world he was. Her Jay. The father of her children. The love of her life. Was now someone new. He was somehow different; someone *else*. She was hoping to formulate her response based on signals from him. But nothing. So she was on her own. There were lots of ways she could go with this. Dismay, disgust at the Wingfields underhandedness, enthusiasm, excitement, intrigue, nonchalance, humor. She went with humor and said, "Well that explains how you got your sexy black hair and swarthy face."

"Swarthy? You think my face is swarthy?" he replied.

"You know what I mean."

"Yeah. You mean that I am swarthy. Like that guy on the Titanic who jumped into the lifeboat with the babies and women. Or Voldemort."

"You are not like Voldemort or Rose's ex-fiancé. His name was Cal Hockley too by the way. And Voldemort was not swarthy. He was actually quite pale."

"He was pale in the movies. Rowling describes him as more reptilian in the book."

"I just need a hug right now."

So Jay hugged her. The sort of hug that people do when they know that as soon as they let go the status quo is over. That life as they knew it is done. So they stayed hugging for a long time because they knew that when they let go they would have to figure out what, if anything, to do.

But with this, this means they have some decisions to make. This means they and their daughters are suddenly part of something. Or could be a part of something. Or should be part of something.

Then suddenly, Jay felt grief. That he was grieving. That he should grieve. He was no longer James Patrick Kirby, Jr. He was someone else. His father was dead. And his death was such a meta-event that he had already lived through as some of meta-spectator and now he was living through it again but differently.

But now who was he?

During a phase Cecilia liked to call his 'parachute phase' because he was clearly trying his best to make her jump, he identified all the cons of marrying him. They included things like: an absurd devotion to the Red Sox, absurd dislike of condiments which would necessitate modified meals for eternity not that you would be making all the meals but to the extent you make meals then the meals you make would need to be modified, three younger brothers could mean three sisters in law to loathe, a preference for lobster over Maryland crabs, a preference for Cape Cod over the Maryland beaches, and issuing offspring would be literally spinning some sort of cosmic lottery wheel. Of course, he also presented her with his list of pros. They included such things as his indomitable wit, his Adonis-like body, his intellect and the limitless earning potential therefrom, he mentioned something about his penis, his thick black hair, the thick black hair surrounding his penis, and the fact that a complete unawareness of his gene pool would make child bearing just that much more adventurous.

He was not certain on what list the fact that he was the only son of JFK Jr., had he known of that fact, would have gone, pro or con.

"Wait. Does Tish – and we will have the Tish conversation at a later date – know who your mother is?"

"Yeah."

"Well who is it?"

"A woman named Gloria."

Shifting Perspectives

He told his parents.

"I'm not sure this new knowledge changes anything." His mother said.

"Yeah but somehow it does" Jay countered.

"I understand what you mean," his dad said. "It's like you are somehow now part of something else."

"Have you addressed this with Tish?" said his mom.

"Yeah. I've gone back and forth with her. I called her and quit. Told her to 'fuck off' and she just told me to cool down and call her when I was ready to talk."

"How can this woman just go around ruining people's lives?"

"Well wait wait wait wait. She didn't ruin my life. She intervened. Maybe interfered. Intruded. Meddled. She just wanted to find out the truth about something. And she did."

"But look what it did to you. Her meddling."

"It hasn't done anything to me, Mom. I haven't done anything yet. And yes, dad, I called her back a couple days ago and yelled at her. She never apologized. Which I admire. And never said something smarmy like 'you should be thanking me' which would be unlike her."

"So you still have a job, then." The dad asked with relief.

"Yes. Still working for them. Still figuring all this stuff out; what this interruption might mean for me. Tish is hard to stay mad at. And even if I were genuinely mad – which I'm really and truly not – I could fake not being mad just to stay close to her. She's a much better person to have as an ally than a foe."

"Who says 'foe'?" teased Cecilia.

Everyone laughed.

"Are you going to get in touch with your mother?" his mom asked.

"I don't know. I think I have to" Jay said. "Tish gave me her name and contact info and she knows that I know. I'm not going to do that to her – not call her."

"Then what? Like are you part of their family now? Like do you get to be on their family tree and in encyclopedias and stuff?" His brother Andrew, who had been silent up to then asked.

"I don't know. I'm sure famous people get this all the time. 'I'm your child. Give me money.' There are surely standard operating procedures in place for it."

"How are you doing, Cecilia?" his dad asked.

"I think I'm fine. I think we're fine. It's like when you ask us how we are doing, we can both respond 'all of the above' because we are both confused and scared; before that we were angry at Tish; then we were happy to finally know; then we thought the whole thing was silly and that nothing changes; and then we felt guilty for being so naïve because everything changes. This cycle repeats itself every couple of hours or so."

"And the girls?"

"We haven't told them yet."

"That's probably smart."

"Thanks."

"Well you've never been a boring child, Jay."

"Thanks Dad. That's a compliment right?"

"One of the best."

Getting ready for bed later that evening, Cecilia said, "accidentally marrying the son that no one knew JFK Jr. had is like that thing when you are stuck in traffic on your way to the airport and as a result, you miss your flight and you are really pissed off but then that flight crashes and you start to wonder and reassess and reevaluate the role of fate and maybe even your whole concept of what it means to be alive."

"Extending that metaphor to its logical conclusion, that means our marriage was destined to be a plane crash."

Cecilia laughed. "Well then let me rethink that, counselor."

After a few seconds of silence, save for the swish-swish of pillow ruffling and duvet cover rustling, she continued, "Jay?"

"Yes honey?"

"Can I tell you something that's been bugging me?"

"Sure."

"You promise you won't get mad?"

"Come on."

"You've been talking about you and this and what this does to you and whether you should contact your mother and whether you should suddenly jump into this Kennedy world; and I've done it too, I've been thinking about me. I just need to hear you say that you know that this decision affects others too. Like this woman. We don't know much about her – but does she want to be contacted? Does she want to know you? Does she want to be on CNN? This is way bigger than us. Even though it's only about us. It's bigger too."

"Yeah I get it. Thanks for sharing. It's easy to lose sight of that. I'm guilty."

"At the same time, it's like how do you not have free reign – how do we not have free reign – to be a little selfish now?"

"Yeah. Is this what famous people do? Like are famous people aware of all the footnotes they leave in their wake?"

"We can't leave footnotes in our wake. I'm even ok not even leaving a wake of any kind."

"Me too."

"I love you."

"I love you too."

"Also, with the plane crash scenario you posit, not being on the doomed plane I was supposed to be on, fate or coincidence or some cosmic accident merely thwarted my demise. This is like a thwarted plane crash that catapults us into some other world."

"What do you mean?"

"Like if we missed catching a flight on a plane that was about to crash, we might not even be aware of it. This is more like sudden fame. Like we are newly rescued Chilean miners suddenly in the spotlight."

"Or that Utah girl who went missing for ten years and then was found again."

"Are you making fun of me?"

"Sort of."

He laughed. Then sighed.

"And Jay, we are not just all a bunch of Mr. Magoos blindly walking around and careening off things, narrowly escaping falling pianos and walking on steel construction beams blissfully unaware that one misstep would result in our own deaths. We are in charge here."

"Yeah. This happens all the time. Little blips and cosmic wrinkles of which we are unaware. Like if I had gotten into Fordham then we might not have met."

"I'm not a philosopher. I'm just tired and a little bit horny."

With that they stopped talking.

PART 5

BREAKERS

Jay emailed Gloria one day in June. Unprompted. Unprovoked. Unplanned. Unannounced. He just wanted to. They began an email exchange. They spoke on the phone a few times and laughed and cried and just took deep breaths and abandoned their respective scripts and agreed that the best way to have the conversations they needed to have was to meet in person.

Gloria told her parents and sister about Jay. It was a three-step process. First, she told Arun her plan to make a surprise visit to Homer and that he could be there if he wanted to be but it was going to be chaos and she really wouldn't be offended if he went somewhere else. Arun said that he would go along, for support, and also so he could enjoy some of Western New York's delicious Apple Cider which is extra good in October.

Second, she gathered her parents, Connie and Dave Greenwood and her sister and brother in the living room and told them that she had a son and his name was Jay. Hearing nothing, she continued, a general description of that first year in Providence and giving birth and Ruth and the orphanage and how Jay had recently found her and they had begun communicating and maybe (hopefully) soon they would be meeting their new grandson. Or biological grandson. Or quasi-grandson. Her parents, as people, especially parents, frequently do, surprised her with their support and acceptance.

Gloria found – almost universally – that relationships sufficiently evolve over time to be nearly new every so many years. She had experienced during her dating period – between birthing Jay and meeting Arun – the urge or the need to ask after three or four dates some variation of "what is this?" A need to label sure but distinguishing between a fling versus a romance versus a potential life mate was more than the need for a label, it was a more substantive need. Every relationship could stand some form of "what is this?" check now and again. Every participant in every friendship, every parent, every sibling, and yes, every romance could benefit from asking the other "what is this?" Gauge its evolution; or devolution; monitor its progress; note that siblings evolved from nemeses to friends with seemingly no warning; parents enjoyed intermittent periods of omniscience; lovers ricocheted between and about being one another's obsessions to annoyances to partners to rivals. Every handshake at every party could lead to anyone to most anywhere, a friend you have for life or a mere hand to hold you while you do a keg stand. It takes time to stop caring about artifice and decorum and being on your best behavior to being your real self. And it takes even more than time to learn who your real self is.

This migt be especially true of parents and kids. There just comes a day when parents stop worrying about what the neighbors might think or whether minor infractions of the flesh will besmirch their children's mortal souls or whether they failed as a parent because their daughter used the library at which she worked as her own private brothel. They don't stop caring *about* the person. They are just happy that the person is alive. And good.

Ironically, or perhaps not ironically and expectedly, her own mother felt the same guilt Gloria had for not intuitively knowing that her own daughter had been suffering. So everyone told the other that they should all just stop feeling bad and guilty for doing or not doing or knowing or not knowing whatever it is they did or didn't do or knew or didn't know. Cool? But parents, also being parents, had a preoccupation with the obscure details that, even if she were to spend hours trying to think of the most obscure impertinent questions a parent could ask, she never would have been able to manufacture their inaugural questions.

"Did Ruth buy a car seat for the ride from the hospital to the orphanage?" her mother asked. "What will Jay call us when he meets us?" she continued. "Jacob, Matthew and Ashley call us Grammy and Grampy still but it seems odd if a thirty-something-year-old man were to start calling us that."

"Especially if he has names for his adoptive grandparents already." Her father added. "Besides, since Jay has children we should be more concerned about the fact that we now have great-grandchildren and what our great-grandchildren might call us."

"Great-grandchildren? Do they even sell cards for great-grandchildren? I haven't seen them in Target but then again I haven't really been looking for them." Her mother, somewhere between elation and exasperation, continued. "And what for Christmas? How old are the girls?"

"Let's take one step at a time. We haven't even met Jay and... what's his wife's name again? Did you tell us her name and have I forgotten it already?"

"I haven't told you yet. It's Cecilia." Gloria said patiently. Though her demeanor reflected more than mere patience. It was gratitude and joy and relief and more joy and more gratitude. It was wonderful. She was home and burden free for the first time in decades.

"How did you get maternity clothes?" her mom continued. "We still have a whole bin full of them from Julie's pregnancies. Julie that reminds me you either have to go those to Wendy or donate them to the Good Will. They are just taking up space."

"Does Jay like to hunt?" her father asked. "I'd love to take another grandson hunting with me. Will he be able to come here this summer? I'd like to meet him before deer season."

This continued, this beautiful, symphonic, meandering, chaotic, rapid commotion of queries related to the minutiae that only parents can care about. They covered everything from appropriate Christmas gifts for adoptive great grandchildren to what size hunting vest Jay would wear to whether or not Jay was allergic to bees the way that Gloria was because if he was then they should bring an EpiPen along with them when they went hunting and did Jay have brown eyes or blue eyes because one of Julie's kids had blue eyes inexplicably and did he have that cleft chin Gloria's father had and what about his ear lobes, Gloria's were attached but most people's weren't and what about Jay's and where did Jay go to college and uh oh that could spell trouble when Boston College played Syracuse in the Atlantic Coast conference basketball tournament but maybe in honor of her new grandson Gloria's mom could get a Boston College sweatshirt and only wear it when Jay was around and did Jay have a Boston accent and when was the last time they had been to Boston oh golly it must have been more than twenty years ago that time they went with Ernie and Vi to go leaf peeping and they tied a whale watch into the trip and a visit to Boston and man those people cannot drive and they are so rude and can Jay drive better than they do and they really hope he's not rude but they will love him even if he is rude and the thing is it's not Gloria's fault "He's not rude, mom and dad. I've spoken with him and he's extremely polite." "And what does he do for a living?" her mom continued. "Oh that's right you said he was a lawyer" she continued without waiting for a reply. "Wow a real live lawyer in the family you could have used him when you got that speeding ticket in Ithaca a few years ago remember that, hon" she said to her husband with playful admonition and "You don't really need a lawyer for traffic court, mom" Julie, who had until this point been silent, interjected with just a little bit too much enthusiasm but no one really noticed and Gloria decided that she would not make a big deal out of it because yes, this must be pretty upsetting for Julie whose role as Greenwood family's top attention getter was unraveling before her very eyes. But it wasn't Gloria's fault. Or was it? Yeah – it was. When you have a baby and don't tell anyone and then thirty five years later come back to Homer and tell everyone then you are directly responsible for the seismic upheaval in the tectonic plates of the family.

The badinage continued until Gloria's mother suddenly stopped, the way a person walking through an amusement park suddenly stops and remembers they left their fanny pack at the disembarkation shelter of the roller coaster they rode two hours ago, and asked, "When are you going to tell us who Jay's father is?"

Which prompted Gloria to begin the process of introducing step three. Step three was telling them about Jay's father. Which would require sufficiently more nuance and delicacy. To put it mildly. To put it very mildly. But she also knew that the degree of their astonishment would be directly proportionate to the amount of suspense she created which would inevitably be directly proportionate to the amount of time she spent preparing them for the announcement. So she just went for it, and as succinctly and declaratively and as matter of factly as was humanly possible, said, "Jay's father is John Kennedy, Jr."

There was silence. And then laughter. And then more silence as her family looked to Gloria mid-laughter and saw that she was neither laughing nor particularly amused by the fact that they were. Then, like when a baseball player hits a ball that everyone knows is going far but they hold their breath until the ball officially make sit past the wall and then when it does the whole stadium collectively and simultaneously exhales and erupts in cacophonous cheer, her family erupted in questions. Most of which were variations on "What do you mean John Kennedy, Jr.?" or questions that were really just statements but with the right inflection of incredulity and shock became questions, like "THE JFK, Jr.?!!" or "The real JFK, Jr.?" or "JFK's son? That JFK, Jr.?" or "JFK Jr. from the magazine?" and variations on that. Gloria finally interrupted when her mother asked, "Are you sure?"

"Yes mother. I am sure that JFK, Jr. is the father of my son, Jay. He was unaware of the fact that I was pregnant and never knew about Jay."

Then she told them the whole story. Which, starting with the rugby shirt and shorts and muddy knees and beautiful pores in the basement of the John Hay library.

She and her sister were not the type of sisters who shared things. They were not the sort of sisters who talked about things like guilt and hope and the adeptness and size of their lovers.

Which was unfortunate because Julie really wanted to know, and Gloria really wanted to tell her.

What Ifs

Gloria and Jay spent a few more weeks emailing; then talking on the phone. Asking each other for details, first the salient details then the ancillary details, of their respective lives. When Jay asked her if his dad *liked her* she knew what he was getting at. She responded with the sort of absolute certainty that assuaged the suspicions he didn't realize he had that John – his dad – might have been a jerk. He wasn't. And Gloria relayed to her son that this wasn't the sort of fling or dare or one night stand of which college boys were so very fond. The way he walked. The way he talked. His authenticity. The complete lack of artifice to him. The gleam in his eyes when he talked about his future plans. And yes, those included politics because how could they not?

She told Jay about the look on his face the first time he saw her. He, while not overtly smitten, clearly thought she was beautiful. He was literally JFK Jr. From the White House; from New York City; from America's royal family. And she was literally Gloria Winegar from Homer, NY, a small village about twenty-five miles south of Syracuse, NY. Where it never ever stops snowing; where people work hard and vote Republican hard and race dirt bikes hard and hunt deer hard and talk about the size of the deer they killed and how many points the antlers of the dead deer had and harvest apples and make apple cider and put the apple cider in barrels and talk about how many barrels they got from their trees and they let the apple cider sit in barrels so that it becomes something more like whiskey than apple cider and they drink the no-longer-apple-cider with their friends in back yards and basements and garages and they challenge the limits of carnivorousness with their omnipresent chicken barbecues and ham dinners and steak dinners and overarching reverence for meat.

He had never been there.

She told him about Ruth. About the night he was born. About the night after the night he was born. About her favorite blanket. About her first concert. Her husband. Her house. They both felt like they had a new friend.

She told him that she could not say, with any degree of absolute certainty, that she had thought about him every single day between September 12, 1983 and today. Nor could she say with absolute certainty that she had not thought of him every day between then and now. That he always just was. Nor could she say for certain that she had or had not thought about John every single day between September 12, 1983 and any given present day. And what did that even mean – to 'think' about him? Would a brief nearly subconscious acknowledgement – something greater than a synapse but something that did not quite rise to the level of cogitation - that mucous-covered child had once slid out of her hoo-hoo be considered a thought? Would that suffice? What about a quasi-Pavlovian sort of sadness that she felt whenever saw a mother and a boy who likely would have been his age – though she was admittedly bad at guessing kids' ages? Would that be a thought? Even if it seemed more biological that intellectual? What if she went to bed and realized with certainty that the human she produced had not crossed her mind in any way shape or form the entire day so she intensely willed herself to do so. But then she realized that by doing so, she was conjuring images in her brain more as a means to eviscerate the guilt she suddenly felt for not producing thoughts in her brain than actually and authentically wondering about who he was and what he was doing. She was certain that there were many days – and these were typically ordinary days that crept on her for reasons of which she was unaware – when she would consciously sit down and make it a point to think about him and do with an intensity that might best be described as prayer – "please let him be happy" and "please let him be healthy" and "please keep him safe" – though it was unclear to what cosmic deity those requests were being made.

Meeting at the Front Portico

She could locate no authority which might provide some semblance of protocol or etiquette for their imminent meeting. There were, she could say with near certainty, no rules to which she must adhere, nothing she must do or say and no proscribed order in which she must do or say it, no guidelines about how to address the other or if either should curtsy or shake hands or hug. If Emily Post had ever opined on the appropriate etiquette for the scenario in which they currently find themselves, they were unaware of such an opinion. Unlike a wedding, there were no guidelines on what fabrics or colors to wear based on time of day and season and whether this might be one's first such meeting or second such meeting. As such, Gloria opted for a Kelly green linen pantsuit. It was a lot of Kelly green but it worked because of her long legs and youthful appearance and good figure. The suit was sophisticated yet fun – more Diane Keaton than Hilary Clinton; more Southampton than Manhattan.

Guys have it easy. He wore a pair of jeans and a plaid blazer.

Even if Ms. Post had provided protocols for this imminent meeting and had she been aware of them, blissfully or non-blissfully, she was rather certain she would have adhered to them in light of the fact that she was nearing 60, and in the process of eschewing all reticence, bashfulness, and restraint – characteristics with which she might have always previously been associated. She was no longer demure.

They already knew so much about one another through their chats and emails. The cadence of their thoughts, their unique senses of humor, their commonalities, their similarities.

They were meeting at the Breakers, a former mansion of the Vanderbilt family in Newport, Rhode Island, his suggestion. Gloria told him that this seemed unfair as it is much closer to her home than his but Jay assured her it would be just fine. He did not tell her that he, still taking advantage of a very and rarely contrite Tish, would arrive there by boat, one of the Wingfield boats. They were meeting at the front door and would then walk to a restaurant. She arrived early and was greeted by a docent. "Welcome to the Breakers, ma'am." He said.

"Thanks Doug."

"How did you know my name was Doug?"

"It's on your ID badge."

"Ahh right. I always forget I'm wearing that."

When Doug asked her who she was waiting for she paused and quickly calculated the benefits of saying something innocuous like "my son" or "a friend" or if she should tell him the truth. She knew that something innocuous and nebulous like "a friend" would suffice. So would "my son." Mothers meet sons in restaurants every day. But given Doug's genuine curiosity she said, "the son I gave up for adoption 38 years ago and haven't seen since. Him. I am meeting him here for the first time." His eyes widened and he smiled and touched her shoulder. She was surprised by and welcomed this. It's so rare for people to touch one another days. Too high risk – what if the person has some sort of glass jaw or shoulder put together with a complex and precarious series of levers and pulleys and your touch shatters it and you get sued. So she liked this. He genuinely cared. She realized she just "The son I gave up for adoption" and realized how cantankerous and Dickensian it sounds. So many consonants creating such harshness in already overly harsh words. Again, let down by Emily Post.

Arun had offered to join her; she said she would be fine and so he was waiting for her at the hotel. He drove her there. Eagerly and lovingly. Her husband was crazy in love with her.

Doug the docent waited with her and it seemed like they both saw him at the same time. "That's him right?" Doug asked.

"Yeah. How did you know?"

"He's by himself and looks nervous. And looks just like you."

At which Gloria started to get choked up.

"You can do this....what's your name again?"

"I don't think I ever told you my name. And I forgot my ID badge." They laughed. "It's Gloria Winegar."

"It was lovely to have met you Gloria. You have a good night."

It was taking Jay forever to walk to the front door. Goddamn Cornelius and his massive front lawns.

"Thanks Doug. You too."

The man who stood before her was taller than he looked in his online photos. And better looking. And looked just like his father. He had the energy of a good man. Gloria hugged him. He cried. She cried. And they stayed like that for many minutes.

Revolving Door

At a restaurant called the Revolving Door, they ordered food, lump crab and shrimp toast; he ordered the Lavender and Miso Glazed Duck Breast with blackberry gastrique and sunchoke puree. She ordered Black Spaghetti with chorizo and mussels. Her new son ordered his food like the sort of person who orders lavender and miso glazed duck breast with great frequency. As though he had been a Kennedy his whole life. He did not inquire or quibble about the sugar content of the blackberry gastrique. Her new son did not order a drink and she wondered if there was a story there. Her new son did not wear socks with his driving moccasins and jeans. All of this – the gastrique, driving moccasins with no socks, the temperance – made her happy.

On the thirty-minute walk from the Breakers to the Revolving Door they asked each other about some eight zillion questions. Where to even begin? On a continuum of queries, which ones are most valuable? Which ones reveal the most about a person? Which ones elicit the most valuable information from the person answering them? Which ones reveal the most about the person asking them?

What's your favorite color? What's your favorite ice cream? What's your wife like? What's your husband like? What are your kids like? What are your hobbies? What music do you like? What's your favorite book? What's your favorite movie? If you could have dinner with any three people living or dead, who would they be?

Eventually they eased into a more conversational cadence. She started with life in Homer; Dave and Connie; Syracuse University; Chester Gillette; Ruth. He then told her all about Sandwich; about Patrick and Rosemary; about hockey and

Sandwich and Boston College and law school; about Cecilia and his daughters and their dog; and Tish. It's easier to tell someone things in person.

She birthed her son on September 12, 1983. Months after Brown University's graduating class of 1983 had thrown their caps in the air and left campus – for the law schools and medical schools and European trips and Wall Street and Madison Ave and all the places for which she had resented the graduates of the Ivy league go; to do the things that Ivy League graduates do. Her friend Ruth Steward helped her birth him. It was a Tuesday and she was back at work on Monday, thanks in large measure to Ruth's care. She was a nurse at Women & Infants Hospital and helped her circumvent some standard operating procedures.

They finished dinner and order dessert. They both order hibiscus panna cotta. Jay asked if they could drive up to Fall River, Massachusetts to see St. Joseph's Orphanage. Gloria said sure and called Arun and told him to meet them at the end of Thames Street.

Arun arrived and met Jay Kirby. They hugged. Her husband hugged her son. Arun drove and Gloria sat in the passenger seat and Jay Kirby sat in back as though he was a child and they had been doing this – driving around in a car – for years. With the windows down.

And having done so, she was certain that she was someone's mother.

Grandpa Dave and Gramma Connie

The next few months were filled with introductions and meetings and walks and visits and more introductions and more navigating new names and more changes.

Gloria traveled to Hingham to meet Cecilia. There was a large banner hanging from the front of their house which said "Welcome Grandma Gloria!" Each letter hand drawn in that way kids do where they underestimate the amount of paper needed to fit the letters and so the last letters get all squinched up. Cecilia met Gloria. Gloria met Lucy and Lillian and Melody. They all said, "Nice to meet you Grandma" in a way that told Gloria that they have been clearly coached on the intricacies of why they were suddenly meeting a third grandmother when they already had two perfectly good healthy ones. Cecilia and Gloria walked along the beach while Arun and Jay worked at home. Cecilia and Gloria went shopping and got ice cream. Gloria was both a new mother-in-law but also not.

Jay and Cecilia and the girls traveled to Homer to meet the Winegars. Jay met Dave and Connie. Connie insisted on giving him some lemonade. Dave had necklaces made of old typewriter keys that spelled the names of each of the girls ready for them. Jay talked hunting with Dave and, while Dave was showing Jay his crossbow, he got choked up when he saw that his grandson had the same knuckles as he did; and the same little bump in their noses. After dinner Dave, Jay and Arun had a cigar on the back porch and it might have been one of the best moments in Dave's life.

270

It's like that thing at weddings when the bride's co-worker dances with the groom's great uncle and you just wonder how and why these people ever happened to be in the same room together and you celebrate and revel in the fact that they are.

The whole summer was like that.

Gloria traveled to Sandwich to meet Jay's parents and siblings. Jay's parents were overcome. With joy. Gratitude. They had lobster. Gloria met Ryan's wife and Rusty's wife and Andrew's husband. They ate and talked and drank and laughed for hours.

Gloria met the Wingfields. She saw the sinister detective who showed up at her house a few months prior pruning hydrangeas. And they hugged again. He really was not such a sinister detective after all.

Everyone hugged all summer. That's all they did.

They wondered if it was inevitable that someday people would learn that Jay existed and that he was the son of JFK Jr. That his face might one day sell a gajillion magazines and books and turn into some sort of frenzy. JFK Jr. has a son. JFK Jr. is a grandpa. But they would cross that bridge when they came to it. And were determined to stay as anonymous as possible for as long as possible. And they did their best to make the summer of 2021 as tranquil as they could. Enjoying the calm before any impending storm. Though they were in uncharted waters as it were. No one really knew what to do.

They had the Wingfields contact someone to talk with Caroline Kennedy and, after the standard DNA testing and so forth, she agreed to meet with them. They met at her mother's home on the Vineyard. Any trepidation Jay might have been quickly eviscerated as Caroline, who one might think would be impervious to shock and emotion and general feeling at this point, broke down as soon as she saw him and was just as kind and enthusiastic and welcoming as could be. She coordinated meetings with his new extended family and met a zillion third cousins.

Corn

People wanted Gloria to tell them about herself. This is something she should have practiced. Or should have practiced more. Or should have taken more seriously when Ruth tried to practice with her . "I'm from a small town in upstate New York" she would begin which sounded so Holden Caulfield. So she pivoted and talked about being an archivist at Brown University. Which many people confused with archaeologist and she loathed the whole occupation thing so she pivoted again and told them about how much she loved eggnog and corn on the cob and *Saturday Night Live.* She was glad when conversation shifted to him. What was he like? By now she knew that everyone knew about the coffin and the stupid bar exam and the Cumberland Island wedding. So she talked about his rugby shirts and pores and his whistling and his kindness and humor.

How many people get judged by a photo taken on their third birthday?

Most of these conversations were with Jay, who needed to make his dad a human, a boy, a man. He researched and investigated and inquisited to discover the person behind the bar exam and the plane and the magazine. He felt oddly connected to him. Though how dissimilar their lives had been. His dad born to a president-elect and his wife, born to a whole world eager for youth; he born under cover of darkness and left at an orphanage.

EPILOGUE

As of this printing, Jay was still deciding what he wants to do. The Wingfields have told him he could be president if he wanted and a still-contrite Tish has promised to support him, back him, bank him. But let's face it, if Jay wants to be president he could be. He wouldn't even have to try that hard. Maybe just make a few bumper stickers. And some posters. He's just that good. He has that rare double benefit of being both an outsider with an asterisk that identifies an absurdly recognizable name with insider pedigree. Apparently, people are yearning for sophistication and comfort and intellect. And they like a story like his. Jay has a new identity to construct. Jay and Cecilia have a tough road ahead of them. A year ago, he was coaching his daughters' soccer teams. And coaxing them into eating vegetables. He was stapling class handouts with his wife. He was negotiating domestic chores with her, offering to go to the grocery store and questioning her reliance on Amazon while she was questioning the fact that he test drove an Audi without telling her first.

But also, after spending time with his myriad Hyannis Port cousins and seeing what *their* life is like, he and Cecilia seem inclined to walk away from it all. They are perfectly fine people – like any time you assemble one hundred people in a group, you are going to find some jerks and some angels and some clowns and some of every single thing – but that sort of life is not always what it seems. They had a pretty amazing existence before. Why waste time with all the bullshit fame would hurl at them?

This is not what Cecilia signed up for, as the saying goes. But then again, who signs up for anything? Who wants guarantees? Sometimes she's sort of into the adventure; leaning into the chaos as it were.

But if you have the opportunity for greatness, like could Jay be great, then shouldn't he take it?

There was this one day, at the apex of all the meeting and the greeting and the introductions, where Jay and Gloria and Arun found themselves sitting together. They had just finished eating in Dave and Connie's garage amidst the holiday decorations and hunting accoutrements and typewriter parts and sports equipment and automobile parts and lawn care equipment and tools of Gloria's youth. Everyone had just finished dinner and they sat there as just the sort of thing where three people inadvertently find themselves together – they had just finished dinner and great Grandma Connie took one of the twins inside to show them her knitting needle collection and Cecilia took Melody inside for a bath and Dave took the other of the twins outside for some sort of hunting tutorial, nearly tripping over himself when she expressed an interest in bow hunting. They were talking about what to do the next day. Cooperstown or Niagara Falls. Dave reentered the garage and muttering to himself asked, "Now what did I do with that range finder and bow hoist?" as he picked around his workbench and hunting cabinet.

"Have a seat, Dave." Arun says. So Dave sits. Arun, pours a glass of wine for Gloria and then he pours a glass of wine for Jay, the grandson of President John F. Kennedy, he gets a beer for his father-in-law, and for himself. And he said, "Cheers to my family." And there they all were. Dave doesn't sit long. He and Connie, with new enthusiasm for exercise and cardiac health, ready themselves for their evening walk. Because if that baby Ruth drove to the orphanage in her Datsun is going to be president of the United States someday; they all want to be around for it. Or maybe, Jay would decide that in addition to his ordinary birth, his ordinary life was just fine.

Gloria surveyed the scene. The four of them, sitting under a single solitary 75-watt light bulb, drinking wine and cheap beer in Dave's garage. Assembled just as haphazardly and inexplicably as all of the hunting accoutrements and snow removal gear and old wool jackets and boots and drill bits and vise grips and croquet sets and badminton rackets in Dave's garage. The four of them just as worn; but just as loved. It was so mystifying to her – all this life that these people generated; all opf the wit and confusion and laughter and sadness. It didn't really make for a great scene or a great drama or many great lines. It really wasn't that great a story, but she loved it anyway.

Acknowledgments

My roommate in college, Meathead, was an accounting major. But after graduating and doing accounting for a year or so, he decided he no longer wanted to account so he moved to New York City to be an actor. It surprised and inspired and amused us, this seemingly abrupt departure from all that we thought we knew about Meathead. He got headshots and was in some off-Broadway plays and an episode of a rather popular TV series and he was Buzz Lightyear at FAO Schwartz for a couple Christmases. He also catered a lot of dinner parties. And regular parties. One early morning or late night, sometime in 1999, when my wife and I lived a few blocks from Meathead on the Upper East Side, we got a phone call, we had only a landline then, and when I answered it, Meathead breathlessly asked, "Are you fucking sitting down, GMA?" And I said something like, "It's 2:30 in the morning, Meaty, I'm laying down." Then this:

"Guess who I fucking saw at this party I worked at tonight?"

"Who?"

"JFK, Jr."

"Fuck you."

"Dude. I swear to God."

"Fuck you Meathead. You're lying."

"Gary, I wouldn't lie to you about this."

We then spent the next hour or so talking about Meathead bartending at a party at which JFK, Jr. also was. I recall Meathead saying, "The first thing I noticed about him was his skin. He had the best-looking skin on any human being I have ever seen." The conversation was peppered with phrases like, "best looking person I had ever seen," "the air just felt different with him in it" and "he just has this presence."

Later that summer, we had our days free as I was teaching high school at the time and Meathead working nights, we went to 20 N. Moore to see the impromptu memorial in front of JFK Jr. and Carolyn Bessette Kennedy's apartment.

So I must thank Meathead who in large measure prompted me to ask the question, what happens to someone when they meet JFK, Jr.?

If you have the means, get yourselves a friend like Meathead who will call you at 2:30 a.m. and talk to you about something he knows you would like to talk about; who shares the same excitement about things you do even though he definitely might not ordinarily share the excitement.

Thanks too to Mario Puzo for manufacturing a Kennedy with his book "The Fourth K" which I bought from WaldenBooks at the Walden Galleria in 1990. Hardcover. It seemed bold, to just create a new Kennedy brother. But why not? Thanks also to Toni Morrison for once saying, "If there is a book that you want to read but it hasn't been written yet, then you must write it." I had always wanted to read a book about JFK, Jr.'s children. Of course, I wanted it to be a work of non-fiction but that doesn't look like it's going to happen. So here's a novel.

Thanks to my family who let me leave the house now and again to write at the library or the coffee place or the beach. Thanks to mom and dad for encouraging and for buying me those Kennedy books when I was in 8th grade. Thanks to those other two infamous Brown alumni Craig and Michelle for reading and answering hundreds of texts about Brown, the cafeteria, the streets, the night life, the library basements, the viscosity of the chocolate milk. Thanks to Kirby Gann for reading drafts of this and being both honest and supportive.

Thanks to everyone I identified in the acknowledgments of my first book, the teachers and the family and the friends. Thanks also to librarians. What they do is amazing. The ladies at the Stevens Memorial Library in Attica, NY helped me so much. When I read all of the Judy Blume they suggested Paul Zindel and when he was all done they suggested Robert Cormier and then S.E. Hinton and then they didn't raise an eyebrow or try to talk me out of reading *The Amityville Horror*.

About the Author

Gary M. Almeter is a writer and attorney who lives in Baltimore, Maryland with his wife, three children, and two dogs, Dave and Mixly. He is the author of the memoir *The Emperor of Ice-Cream.*

More from Gary M. Almeter

About the Press

Unsolicited Press was founded in 2012 and is based in Portland, Oregon. The press produces stellar fiction, nonfiction, and poetry from award-winning writers. Learn more at www.unsolicitedpress.com.